Messy

Corola De Rosa

A Food Freaxxx novel
by

Corola De Rosa

Messy

Food Freaxxx Book 1

Published by Pastelito Publishing LLC

Cover illustration and design by Andrée-Anne Mercier
Photograph of cake by Becky Merbler
Cake by Confections PGH
Book formatting by Erik Gevers

ISBN ebook: 979-8-9988603-1-7
ISBN paperback: 979-8-9988603-0-0

Content Warning

This book contains depictions of food being fetishized and interacted with in ways other than eating.

for the decadent queers of Pittsburgh and beyond

1

Vic's Dog Days

I'm working the flower section first today. My eyes rove over the other penciled-in tasks I've been assigned for today's shift, but I'm no longer seeing the long, scroll-like sheet on the clipboard that hangs from the massive customer service desk. Instead, I imagine how he might stop by today and spot me in the flower section, ask me to pick out whichever bouquet I wanted for his apology offering. I'd throw my arms around his neck and plant a big wet one on him, right then and there, in my bright, flowery uniform t-shirt. I'd take him back in a heartbeat.

I release the day's schedule and huff out a sigh. Dee sidles up beside me, clocking in three minutes late like she always does.

"Oh, God." Dee rolls her eyes at me. She is tall and slender, her sandy blonde-brown hair cut into a short shag. She has light eyes and a penchant for wearing bolo ties, even and especially with her store uniform and on days we have derby bouts. She's also the only person I know who wears— who can stand to wear— high-top canvas sneakers at work.

I glance sidelong at my best friend. "What?"

"I heard that sigh. Guess I have to deal with Lovesick Vic all shift."

Now I roll my eyes. "So sorry my shitty breakup is an inconvenience to you."

"Wow, no wonder you're the customer favorite. That was so believable!" Her sarcasm makes the corners of my lips quirk up despite my mood. She punches me in the shoulder and traipses off to whatever section she's been assigned to first—produce, probably.

I don't hate our customers. I'm just over customer service in general. I've had the job for about five years, and about two years in I started to feel really weird about the level of subservience required to work in customer service.

A lot of things built up over time to bring me to this point, like my friends pointing out that I apologize constantly. It's become totally second-nature for me. "Sorry, the organic crunchy peanut butter is out of stock due to supply-chain issues." "Sorry, the hibiscus banana bread is seasonal." Leaching into my personal life, this turned into, "Sorry I forgot to look at the takeout menu before coming over." It feels like soon I'll be saying, "Sorry I exist."

For others, for customers especially, the grocery store I work at is an *experience*. For me, it's like stepping into the home of my least favorite extended family member, familiar yet grating. The store is a public place, but as my workplace, there's an intimacy there, too, a comfortable, settled feeling when I move through the store on brisk, booted feet. Online and in the media, people often refer to the store's vibe as "fun and funky," and the particular effect of that vibe wore off on me after about a year. You get used to it. It loses its charm, its shine. I think it's hard for anyone to find their workplace charming after that initial honeymoon phase.

Time goes by fast when working a closing shift. After a couple of hours spent condensing the remaining flowers in preparation for the arrival of tonight's order, the familiar call-out rings through the aisles like the canon of a children's song: "Truck's here!" My coworkers echo the words as soon as they hit their ears, spreading the word throughout the store. It brings me out of the spiraling reverie I haven't let go of since clocking in. He's not coming to perform some grand romantic gesture at my place of work today. He's not going to risk bumping into me by shopping here when he knows I'm scheduled to work. He's never coming back to me.

I'm grateful for the familiar process of breaking down the newly delivered pallets for the frozen section, which I lead. Our chain of stores is known for our convenient, yummy frozen foods. The situation is time-sensitive, not wanting these items to defrost (health hazard) or for the cardboard to become soggy (gross). It's important to stock the coffins— the official term for the long, open, horizontal display rectangles of frozen product— and get whatever doesn't fit in the coffins put away as back-stock as quickly as possible.

Once I'm done unloading the pallets and getting boxes onto flat carts for my coworkers to stock product on the sales floor, I station myself in the storage freezer, mostly immune to the cold in my hoodie and gloves, except for my sniffling nose. I need a ladder to reach the tallest shelf, and by the end of "working the load," as we call it when we unload and organize the truck delivery, I have boxes squished against the ceiling. As I work to jam all the back-stock into the storage freezer, I wonder briefly if I ordered too many margherita pizzas, but they usually sell pretty well.

The hours until we close go by fast once we start working the load. Soon, the aisles are devoid of customers and it's just the crew stocking shelves, talking shit. After we stage everything, stacking boxes to the right of the empty-ish shelves the boxes' product will fill, I man my usual starting point for stocking. I always start at the jars of pasta sauce. There's something so satisfying to me about stocking these particular shelves, a few somethings actually: I like how easy their boxes are to break down, I like the dull clink the jars make when they bump into each other, and, since they're a popular item, there's always plenty of product to work— usually a stack of cases taller than I am.

A couple of other friends and coworkers populate this aisle; dry goods always has a lot of product to restock at night. Dee is beside me working on apple sauces and peanut butters. Like me, she's a lifer. She started working here about a year before I did and made quick work of befriending me after being assigned to train me for a couple days when I was hired. As a general rule of thumb, lifers have been working at the store for five or more years— long enough to make it pretty difficult to leave due to seniority benefits, the sunk cost fallacy, and the ease with which we complete tasks simply because of our wealth of experience on the job. Outside of work, Dee and I spend a lot of time together while practicing or hanging out with our derby team, and beyond that, we hang out one-on-

one as friends quite a bit.

We started roller derby at the same time because we made a pact one day while working produce together, both confessing it as something we'd always wanted to try. Neither of us had put on a pair of skates since we were kids, and we were both terrified in our own ways to try a sport that would require us to sprint on skates and get really physical with others while wheeling around.

We were pleasantly surprised to find the local derby league very welcoming of newbies, willing to train anyone who wanted in on this particularly intensely committed hobby... as long as we proved ourselves to be as intensely committed as the current members. This is no small feat, but Dee and I were up to the task, as we had plenty of pent-up violent frustrations (mostly work- and society-related) that were best expressed on the track. I leaned into the cathartic rage so much that I dubbed myself with the derby name Vicious Vulva.

"I think we have a chance at taking home the big trophy at Hairy Pitts this year," Dee says as she rips into the plastic shrink-wrap on a case of crunchy organic no-stir peanut butter. "Hairy Pitts" is the once-unofficial, now official-due-to-popular-use name of the big derby tournament in our region. The name is a silly portmanteau derived from the first teams to face off in the regional tournament fifteen years ago: Harrisburg and, yours truly, Pittsburgh. Teams from all over Pennsylvania, Ohio, and West Virginia compete for spots at the big tournament.

Our team, the Barbedbies (like barbed wire Barbies— I know, it takes a second but it has grown on me and we really love a portmanteau in this sport), is good enough that we have made it into Hairy Pitts a few times over the years—once during my tenure— but on the off years we don't make it, and also have to host here in the Burgh, it really makes us all sore as fuck. This year, taking home "the big trophy" as Dee aptly puts it, will be extra difficult because we won't have the home turf advantage. The tournament the city is held in rotates throughout our region each year, but this year, it will be in Harrisburg. The trophy is really fucking big. A favorite winning team tradition is for the women to take a photo huddled around the trophy, teammates stacked one on top of the other like kids in a trench coat, the approximate height of the trophy.

"It's only April! Hairy Pitts is still like, four months away," I tell Dee, shaking my head.

"I know, but we've been killing it during our pre-season practice sessions. I'm calling it now: We're leaving a path of destruction in our wake this season."

"Down, girl," I say, laughing. "Play nice."

"Never!" Dee declares, holding the last jar of organic crunchy no-stir above her head for emphasis, seemingly as some kind of sacrifice or weapon, I'm not quite sure. My bestie is a little off her rocker and I love her all the more for it. Her enthusiasm gives me hope for the season.

At home after my shift, the couch is too comfortable. It's too spacious, a vast expanse covered in second-hand stains, and I have it all to myself. Usually, there's a little dollop of white fur invading my space, and a handsome man who I took for the love of my life to share the rest of the couch.

I adopted my little Maltese, Ollie, from a rescue about five years ago, and until six months ago, I lived my life largely by his schedule. Ollie healed me in ways I didn't know I needed to be healed, trained me and taught me the importance of stepping outside every day, however briefly, on our walks. It felt so good to care for that little critter, to know he trusted me to take care of him, to always be there for him. Shame spikes me through the middle. *Not anymore. I'm not there for him anymore.*

Chasing the shame, my mind drags me down Memory Lane to the literal sidewalk where I met the handsome man who used to take up the other half of my couch, while out on a walk with Ollie. (Well, not *this* stained piece of crap I inherited from the previous tenant of this sad apartment. *Our* couch.) Alan didn't have a dog, just enjoyed going for walks and petting other people's dogs. Initially, I found his stereotypical elder millennial manner of being around dogs annoying. He called Ollie a "doggo" and didn't even ask to pet him, which made me roll my eyes. But, unlike other stereotypical doggo-obsessed millennials who grew up during the further side of the 90's, once he straightened up from his squatting dog-booping position, he addressed me, rather than just running off with the can-i-haz-pets oxytocin. Usually people our age just greet Ollie, give him pets, and continue about their obliviously chipper way. Alan actually stopped to chat, the charming, well-intentioned bastard.

I remember he was flirty right out of the gate, immediately endearing me with his Pittsburgh accent, another unusual trait for people our age. All my friends who are from here trained themselves to hide the Yinzer accents they inherited from their parents, buried deep under a mountain of needless Appalachian shame, so the Steel City drawl could only be coaxed out by one too many IC Lights or Iron Beers. That day he pet Ollie for the first time, Alan directed his kind eyes at me confidently and said, "I've seen yinz around while riding my bike. I live down the street. I know you're usually in and out pretty quick, but do you wanna join me for a walk?"

That week, the three of us walked together every day. Half an hour on Tuesday turned into an hour on Thursday and two hours on Saturday.

Today, sitting in my basement apartment with almost nothing to mark it as mine— including a month-to-month lease— I wonder if they went for a proper walk, or just a short in-and-out from the charming old apartment-converted mansion where we all lived together as a happy little family. I'm sure they did go for a proper walk. Alan was— is— an amazing dog dad. I wonder if they miss me, I hope they miss me. In an effort not to cry, I grab my phone and pick up where I left off scrolling, sinking into the lonely couch.

I can't remember the last time I went for a walk. Usually, I'm too tired from working at the store. I'm on my feet all day there. Sometimes I hope Alan will come into the shop. He grew accustomed to all the special items I'd bring home from work, the ones you can't get at the other grocery stores, not for as reasonable a price, anyway. My stomach grumbles at the thought of those specialty items.

I take a deep breath and heave myself off of the couch to make one of my favorite comfort meals. Post-midnight dinners don't bother me much anymore, but I am loath to cook anything complicated after my shift, no matter what time it ends. I'm tired and my body hurts.

In my section, we sell a convenience that has spoiled me to no end ever since I started working at the store: frozen single portions of rice in a bag. All they need is to be microwaved for three minutes, and they turn out perfect every time. A bowl of this rice with two fried eggs over top is one of my favorite meals in the world, a straight-up comfort meal I can't live without, basic as it is.

I leave the pan in the sink after serving my eggs atop my rice and sprinkling them with a little salt and pepper, deciding that the pan is a problem for tomorrow me. I sit on the couch, turn on the TV for background noise. As I break the egg open with my fork, I smile at the perfect doneness of the yolk, now running into my rice. The simple sensuality of it cheers me up a bit and makes me realize that I haven't checked Food Freaxxx in awhile, and I figure, why not. *Dinner and a show,* I think to myself.

Food Freaxxx is part old-school message board, part social media site, part porn bank, part paid exclusive club. Recently, they even launched a (rather buggy but passable) app. It's not exactly a dating app, but it's also not *not* a dating app. It's an online community of people with food fetishes. Most of the time, we share in that sexually platonic/platonically sexual way that is so natural and particular to the internet. Comments of

Mmm I'd love to lick the icing off those pretty titties followed effortlessly by private messages like, **Hope things are going better at work** are commonplace interactions. We're friends who fuck each other through the internet, co-imagining gloriously indulgent, hedonistic, and messy scenarios with the foods we find most sensual. I've gotten to know a few of these gorgeous people quite well, though only by their screen-names and nicknames, and never in person. My FoodFreaxxx screen-name is Vicious Vulva, same as my derby name. We're a small, niche community that's spread out all over, mostly in the US but some of us international. Though it's fun, there's been a bit of a plateau in activity recently. Not too many new members the last few months and things have felt a little stale in the group (pun always intended), but at least there's a sexy new photo or video of one of my friends making a mess of themselves at least once a day.

I scroll through the latest posts as I eat, taking my time with each image and video clip. Today was a particularly fruitful day, it seems. I lick the yolk from my lips as my eyes take in sticky red jam on bouncing, jiggling tits and golden confiture being licked off of hard cocks. Another video shows a dollop of whipped cream with a bright red, shiny strawberry perfectly, delicately balanced atop another perky penis. A graceful hand from off-camera swoops in and gently plucks the strawberry, then swipes it hungrily into the cream. The camera follows the hand and reveals a familiar face, my friend, @Creamy365 which means the pretty penis on camera belongs to @Creamsicle69, her husband, whose point of view I'm inhabiting, since he's holding the camera. I watch her first lick the strawberry gingerly, teasingly, then take a big bite, leaving only the leafy head pinched between her graceful fingers.

Creamy has a beautiful mess of long, golden curls, which she now swiftly gathers into a hasty bun. With her hair out of the way, she leans forward, wraps her pink lips around Creamsicle's cock, sucks and licks it clean. The clip ends there, only about a minute long, short as many of the videos on Food Freaxxx are. It's sensual, it's indulgent, it's art, it makes my pussy warm and wet. I comment, **Yummy!!! You 2 are inspiring meee** and head to the kitchen to see what might lend itself for some sexy content for my internet friends.

I have whipped cream in the fridge. You can never go wrong with whipped cream— it's a classic— but it's not quite what I'm craving right now. I'm feeling a little extra on-edge, like I have something I need to release, and my mood is calling me to be a little more creative. I thought about Alan a little too much today, kept glancing toward the flower section, kept thinking I'd see him walk through the ever-clouded glass of the automatic sliding doors. That maybe he'd have Ollie tucked under one arm, grocery store rules be damned. I need to get out of my head.

I open the freezer and inspiration strikes. My gaze focuses on a box of mini ice cream sandwiches, the cookies-and-cream kind that have a soft, embossed chocolate cookie on either side of the creamy vanilla middle. I grab the box and head back to the living room to set up.

Setting up for filming this type of content has become a sort of sexy ritual for me. It's a kind of solo foreplay to the solo pleasure I'm about to engage in.

Since I expect the mess I'm about to make to be pretty contained, I opt for the softer, mess-friendly waterproof blanket I have for such occasions, rather than the plastic tablecloth I sometimes lay out for my messier sexy messes. I spread the blanket on the floor and push out the thought that, if Ollie were here, he'd be coming over to investigate what I'm doing on the floor. *Floors are for dogs!* his wagging tail would seem to say, his paws on my bended knees, leaning into me with excited curiosity.

I push the thought out of my mind, saunter over to the record player and put my treasured Bongzilla record on, *Gateway*. As the drums and guitars and voice samples pulse into the room, I light the fuzzy bowl I packed into my glass pipe and puff on it, letting the familiar haze warm me.

I have a cheap, four-foot-tall tripod with a flexible neck, which I position near where I will lay my head, holstering my phone onto it in a bird's-eye-view position, the screen facing toward me so I can watch myself. I love watching myself. I love imagining others watching this later, watching me, getting off on the little show I am about to put on.

As the music and the weed wash over me, I feel myself loose something from deep within, feel myself go soft and hot under my own nonjudgmental gaze reflected on the phone screen positioned above me. I take a moment to study my mirror image on the screen. The person I see there looks settled, comfortable. From my core, a wordless sensation amounting to *It's time to play*, rumbles within me.

I grab two mini ice cream sandwiches from the package I set down on the blanket beside me, level with my right hip. I set one on my abdomen just below my breasts and bite the smile on my lips in response to the feel of the cold cookie on the surface of my skin.

The other cookie I split apart. I slip the creamless half into my mouth and show the other half to the camera as I chew, then set the cookie directly onto my nipple, ice cream side down. The cold sensation steals a delicious, hissing inhalation of breath from between my teeth, then I repeat with the other cookie.

I feel their centers start to melt on my skin instantly. I settle the index and middle finger of my hands on each cookie, pressing them softly into my nipples, the pressure intentionally delicate so as not to break the small dark circles. I begin to move the cool, creamy cookies into a slow, swirling motion, the spirals widening to the edge of my areolas, outward, following the roundness of my breast until there's no ice cream left to melt.

I pop each cookie into my mouth. As I chew, I play with the sticky, shiny residue on my breasts, poking and tapping my fingers into my softness, relishing the sticky cream. Once I've eaten the cookies, I go to work licking as much of that sweet stickiness off of me as I can, watching myself indulge on the phone screen, grabbing fistfuls of my breasts to shove into my eager mouth, rubbing my thighs together in *want*.

Once I've licked myself as clean as I can, I stop the recording and head to the shower to finish myself off with my trusty purple waterproof vibrator, excited to edit my little video and post it for my fellow Food Freaxxx to enjoy.

2

Gabby's Confession

We've been together a long time, long for a couple as young as we are. I know everything there is to know about him. Sometimes I think I know him better than he knows himself.

My Darius. I don't regret a moment of the seven years we've spent together, and I honestly love to think how it's just a drop in the bucket compared to how long we still have left to go. We're only 26, and though there are many uncertainties that keep me up at night, whether or not Darius and I have what it takes to make it as a couple is not one of them.

Since the beginning, it's felt so right. His hand in mine, his eyes locked with mine, our laughs winging the air around us together. And the sex isn't too shabby, either. Okay, it's mind-blowing, and it just keeps getting better. Practice makes perfect, as they say.

Ostensibly, today is a typical lazy Sunday for us. We're at our favorite diner, Nancy's in the East End of Pittsburgh. It's a cozy-crowded place with decades of loyal customer photos taped lovingly, if haphazardly, on its teal walls. Behind the front counter, a kitschy brown vintage wallpaper with a chaotic yellow trim at the top greets us every time we walk in. Before I dig into my meal, I make eye contact with the print of Rosy the Riveter on the back wall. On the table in front of me are two of my weekend breakfast favorites: crepe-thin pancakes with crispy edges (a lesser-known Pittsburgh specialty) and scrambled eggs to balance my sweet and savory cravings, plus all the coffee I can drink. For Darius, an omelet as big as his head with as much meat as they can pile on. No coffee for him, though. He loves to tease me by bragging about how he makes it through life without a drop while "everyone" (me) seems to depend on the stuff. He has never liked it, both the taste and the rush of caffeine. Sure, he does black tea now and then, but just for the flavor and nostalgia of his childhood, not because he'll turn into a monster without caffeine like I do.

It still amazes me that he doesn't need caffeine to function. Though I'm not delusional enough to deny my dependence, growing up Cuban-American in Miami makes my coffee habit culturally defensible. Plus, I love the ritual in the morning. But I'd be lying if I said I don't need at least one cup when I first wake up just to feel human. I blame capitalism.

He's a fast eater, I'm slow. He looks at me over his empty plate and sighs contentedly. "What's on the agenda for today?"

I am definitely the planner in this relationship, and I usually have something fun up my sleeve. It's something Darius often says he loves about me. Today, though, his casual question turns the food I've just swallowed into a tumultuous churn in my stomach. Suddenly, I don't want to take another bite. There's something on my mind today, something big, and I have my heart set on telling Darius about it.

Recently, I've started to question my sexuality, and I'm pretty sure I'm bi. Logically, I don't think coming out will be a problem in the slightest, but emotionally, I'm worried Darius will look at me differently. I haven't fully processed what identifying as bi means for me personally, how I view myself. I'm not even sure if it's an identity I should get to claim. I've only ever been with two men— Darius, and my high school sweetheart Javier right before him.

I'm nervous, but this is Darius. He is the love of my life and my best friend on the face of the earth. I look up from my plate to meet his big, dark eyes, framed with the most beautiful, unfair eyelashes, long and thick. I manage a little smile. "I thought we could go for a walk through Frick Park."

"Aw, we should have brought Mimi," Darius laments.

My smile widens and the rising tide in my stomach lowers a bit. "I knew you were gonna say that. But if she came, we wouldn't have been able to come here for breakfast."

"Mimi is a person!" Darius protests. "She's just trapped in a dog's body." I laugh and shake my head. He's my best friend. We know each other like we know ourselves. I take a deep breath, decide against finishing the last few bites of pancake left on my plate so as not to challenge the stamina of the gymnast apparently performing sequential somersaults in my stomach. I drain the last bit of my coffee. Then, we're on our way to Frick Park.

Frick Park is the largest green space in Pittsburgh. There are countless trails we can take, but our favorite is the one that starts out by the bowling greens. The first time we went to that part of the park together, an elderly woman overheard me marveling at the space. "The bowling greens are one of the park's best kept secrets and we'd like to keep it that way," she said to us, and gave me a sassy wink. I don't have the first idea of what lawn bowling is all about.

Darius parks my car along the curb that frames the field at the entrance to this part of the park. The bowling green is occupied by a group of elderly folks, and I wonder if the sassy winker is among them. We head in the opposite direction, though, towards the trail. The treetops are bright with spring green and I find my brain tingling with the unmistakable thaw I experience after each Pittsburgh winter, like I'm waking up from hibernation.

"I wonder if the chipmunks will be out today," I say excitedly.

"I'm sure we'll see at least one," Darius says.

"I never get tired of seeing them scurry all over the place. Do you think I'd feel the same way if we'd grown up with them?"

Darius shrugs. "I don't know. They're pretty damn cute, I think it would be tough to ever find them boring." We both grew up in South Florida, so we have the same frame of reference for these things. We don't bat an eyelash at a gecko or garden snake or ibis, but chipmunks bring out the childlike wonder of two adults slowly growing accustomed to "The North" as we call it.

We moved here from Miami five years ago for me to attend graduate school, Darius ever the supportive partner. I was offered a scholarship to earn my Master's in Fine Arts in creative writing, specifically writing poetry at the University of Pittsburgh. I'm grateful to not have student loan debt, but my degree in the current job market has done me a fat lot of good in these few years post-graduation.

When we came to Pittsburgh, we had no intention to stay. It was intended as an adventure, a fun interlude to experience a new place, but we quickly found ourselves enamored with the city's personality: its bridges, its people, its grit. And, as lifelong residents of the Miami metropolitan area, we had inverse sticker shock at the relative reasonable cost of living (though, like everywhere, that has risen since we first arrived).

I see more reasons for us to put down roots here than not, though homesickness is very real at times, especially when craving any of the pastelitos or other Cuban delicacies I'm accustomed to having a short drive away whenever we're back in South Florida. I have perfected a few of my abuela's recipes, though, and food is Darius' métier; he can make anything my heart desires and often indulges me with just that. Unlike me, Darius loves his job, and we love this city, so for now, we stay.

We walk along the trail in quiet for a while. Darius seems perfectly at ease, but with each step we take, my doubt grows. Doubt about whether I should tell him. Doubt that I'm even bisexual. Doubt that he'll take it as well as I want to believe he will. In the years we've been together, I've admitted to Darius that I've questioned my straightness, of course, but I've never tried to think too hard about it, much less label it. Whenever I've questioned aloud, it's always been low-stakes ("Mulder and Scully are both so hot, ugh!") or hypothetical ("Maybe if we ever broke up, I'd try dating women").

My recent change of heart has come from my favorite para-social relationship. This super-cool, polyamorous lesbian who goes by @Poly_Polly on social media has totally rocked my world. Her content covers everything from figuring out if you're queer when questioning, to leaning into your vanity, to self-pleasure, to how to propose a threesome with your partner. Her content always resonated with me, and until recently, I thought it was just because I was a really empathetic ally to the LGBTQIA+ community. Then, this month, as I voraciously consumed more and more of her content, I found myself wondering if the reason so many of her posts rang true was because I might actually be part of the "B" in LGBTQIA+.

Suddenly, I don't want to stall any longer. I feel like if I have to take another step without saying something, I just might burst. I've never lied to or kept anything from Darius. I can't bear to be anything but one-hundred percent honest with him, always, and it goes both ways. It's always been that way with us. We place honesty and trust above all else in our relationship. "Honey, there's something I want to talk to you about," I blurt.

"What's up?" His tone is casual, not dismissive but easy, inviting. He keeps his eyes on the trail ahead but I know I have his full attention. The birds sing, unaffected by and unaware of my anxieties, but winding the tension within me tighter with their chirps.

My steps, and my speech, falter. "It's kind of serious, but also not a big deal. I don't know."

He's a few steps ahead of me, so I hurry to catch up and grab his hand as though my life depends on it. Darius looks down at me and brings his big, bushy brows together in an expression of concern. "Why are you freaking out?"

"There's just something I want to tell you, and I'm really nervous about it even though it feels silly to be nervous to tell you anything." The words are pouring out of me faster than I can think, like smoke from a burning building. Now I'm worried that if I stop talking I'll never tell him, so I let my worry fan the flames and let the words burn my mouth as they spill out. "I think I'm bisexual." It's the first time I've said it aloud to anyone, and it hurts so good. It feels as true as any other aspect of my identity, but also impossible to prove and scary. I find myself wondering in the back of my head why I said bi-*sexual* instead of just *bi*. Why does it have to feel so explicit, why does it make me feel so naked? Why did I say I *think* I am? Before the momentum can escape me, I correct myself. "I *am* bisexual."

Darius slows to a stop, and I do the same, standing beside him, holding my breath. He turns to me, the two of us facing each other in the middle of the dirt path. "Honey, it's okay." He pauses, gazes into my eyes thoughtfully. "I'm sorry you felt so nervous about telling me. You know you can share anything with me, right?"

"Yeah." My lungs inflate again as I feel my eyes stinging in response to the sincerity in his voice. I can see in his dark eyes that he's a little hurt that I was so anxious about sharing this with him. "I don't know why I was nervous. It just feels like a big change, even though nothing is actually changing."

"That's the beauty of our relationship. We're definitely not the same kids who fell in love in college." He surprises me with his wisdom. He always does when he drops little truth-bombs like that.

"No. You were a lot more dramatic and moody back then," I tease.

"Shut up," he says, then leans down to kiss me. After all these years, I still find his kisses both intoxicating and grounding, like I'm fully in my body, but if I wanted to, I could take off into flight. I can't help myself— I part my lips and let my tongue out to invite him for more. He accepts, and just like that, we're making out in the woods like a couple of horny college students. As I wrap my arms around his neck and feel myself getting lost in him, I hear the sound of footsteps scuffing against the trail. We part, and I look back to see another couple and their big, shaggy dog coming down the hill behind us.

I smile sheepishly as if they can tell what we've been up to, and pull Darius down the trail with an extra-energized spring in my step.

We walk in the happy, quiet chitter of nature, birds singing, the ever-novel chipmunks we love scurrying against bark and ground, Darius taking the lead again with his long, Ent-like steps.

Picking up the conversation as though there has been no lull at all, without missing a step, Darius announces, "I'm bi, too."

There's no mistaking what he's just shared, so I don't bother to clarify or do a double-take. I speed up my walk to move directly in front of Darius and start to walk backwards with him, matching his pace. "Baby!" I squeal.

"What?" He does his best to mimic my high-pitched tone and waggles his head playfully from side to side.

I slow my pace, forcing him to do the same from my backward position in front of him, then reach my hands out for him to hold, our steps now falling in time with each other. "I love you,"

I tell him.

"I love you, too." I move back to his side, wrap my arm around his hips, and lean into him as we continue our walk down the path together.

3

Darius' Unknown Parts

Nothing surprises me, especially not when it comes to Gabby. Maybe that is arrogant, but I don't care because it's true. Somewhere in my early twenties, I started to not give a fuck about things like appearing arrogant. I only care about what is true in this world, and the people I love in it. That's it.

It's beautiful outside. I love walking through nature with Gab, I could listen to her talk all day, and I often do. My inability to be shocked by anything has rubbed off on her a bit over the years, so I relish the look of surprise on her face accompanied by adorable squealy giggles when I repeat the confession she made just moments ago, but this time in reference to myself.

I've known I'm bi for years, but I don't really think about it much. Gabby has been the keeper of my whole heart— and body— for seven years now. But, her confession stirred something in me. It was a welcome reminder that my sexuality isn't about who I'm with, but rather, is part of who I am. So I told her.

"How are we so in sync?" She marvels at me, walking backwards and trusting me to guide her, our fingers interlocked in a soft wrestling gesture.

"Didn't you know? I'm actually Justin Timberlake," I say, deadpan, but cringing internally at my own terrible joke.

"Shut up!" She laughs and my heart fills with the sunlight filtering down from the full, green treetops. Then, her expression turns thoughtful and she asks me, "When did you know?"

"Did you know Wally Short in high school?"

"Yeah," she draws the word out, making it flare up a few octaves.

"We had calc together," I say by way of explanation, shrugging.

"You had a crush on *Wally?* We had French together!" She giggles. "Oh my god, can I *tell* him?"

"What! No, absolutely not," I say, chuckling despite myself. "Wait, are you still in touch with him?"

Now she shrugs. "He was my French buddy! He's still extremely cool and smarter than everyone."

"You so get my type, babe," I poke her in the ribs and she yelps and hops into her next step.

I fell in love with Gabby at first sight. At least, that's how it feels to me. Even though we went to the same high school, we didn't know each other then. Though I'm sure we saw each other in the halls, I never *saw* her until the day she *recognized* me on the college campus of FIU, where she and my friend Ayan studied as undergrads while I sweated my way through culinary school, sometimes through pores I hadn't even known existed. Ayan, an old friend of mine, was a mutual friend of hers. They had gotten to know each other in our senior year of high school.

Ayan and I had known each other since we were kids. We bonded over having some shared experiences as Middle Eastern Americans, his background Lebanese, mine Persian. Though Persians are in fact not Arab, Ayan and I would joke to get through as we got lumped together by our peers, who wouldn't understand the first thing about the Arabization of Iran, which my dad lectured me on since before I had the attention span for it.

Ayan was a stern judge of character, so when I met Gabby through him, I instantly liked her. If she was alright by him, she was alright by me. I trusted his judgment of people that implicitly, that deeply. Being a trio in those days was fun.

Gabby and I had a falling out with Ayan the year after the two of them graduated college, while I was already working my first broiler gig. I still think about him from time to time. Sometimes he even joins the boys online to play video games, but we don't talk too much or too deeply on those rare occasions. He seems like he's doing well, and I'm happy for him. Whoever he was back when we were close— whoever *I* was back then— I've accepted that we're not those people anymore, and I'm okay with those people and that friendship staying in the past.

Regardless of a tough and sad ending to that friendship, I'm grateful to him for linking me and Gabby together, and I always will be.

So, on that fateful day on the FIU campus, I was laying on a bench under a palm tree when she recognized me as Ayan's friend. I was on campus waiting for him to get out of class so we could grab a bite, as a matter of fact. I remember being lost in thought over whether I was missing out on something by not going the collegiate route (I decidedly wasn't). She called out my name incredulously, pulling me from my musings, as if she didn't believe the serendipity of running into me there (despite the fact that the FIU freshmen starting that year from our high school's graduating class numbered in the dozens). I don't know why she was so excited to see me, but the genuinely stoked expression on her face really hit me in the gut. That first noticing, the first time I really *saw* her, I fell in love.

And now, walking in the city woods of Frick Park, hand in hand, revealing unknown parts of ourselves to each other, I fall in love all over again.

4

Gabby's Familiar Places

It's only a ten-minute drive back to our apartment in Squirrel Hill, but it feels like an eternity.

The way Darius opened up to me, and the way he kissed me on the trail took me back to our college days, when our nature walks would get a little dirtier than one might ordinarily expect. I remember one particular instance when passersby almost saw my tits out. I was living out a wood nymph fantasy I didn't even know I had.

Even though my body was ready to risk it all in the middle of Frick Park, my brain knows better. I'm not opposed to exhibitionism, but it's sure as hell not going to be in the middle of a family-frequented nature trail on an uncharacteristically sunny Pittsburgh-April-Sunday afternoon.

I can tell Darius is struggling to keep his full focus on the road as he drives my beat-up sedan. He keeps shooting hungry looks in my direction, his dark eyes devouring me every time we hit a little spot of traffic or a red light. Just now, as the light we're sitting at turns green, he pats my thigh and gives it a possessive squeeze. I laugh. "Pay attention to the road!"

"I'm looking at the road," Darius protests. "I'm just resting my hand on this comfy armrest." He rubs my thigh, the "comfy armrest," for emphasis.

"Mmm." I'm tempted to peel his hand off of me, to tell him to be responsible and put both hands back on the steering wheel, but I can't bring myself to lose his touch. Instead, I layer my manicured hand over his and rub the back of it with my palm, pressing him into my thigh, hating the cute pants I'm wearing because they're a barrier to his naked touch. My bright orange nails look so pretty against the sky-blue fabric, though.

Our one-bedroom apartment is on the third floor of a hundred-year-old building that is shaped like a horseshoe. It's nothing grand, but we make it work. The kitchen and living room are spacious enough, and I've tried to make it homey with thrifted and vintage furniture and knickknacks. We even have a sunroom that overlooks the building courtyard, where I do my writing when the mood strikes me and continuously try to keep a handful of plants alive.

When we arrive home, Mimi, our black and white pitbull mix, is beside herself with excitement that we're home. I make sure to pee right away, after hanging my jacket on the hook by the door. Since I am prone to urinary tract infections, I always pee before and after sex (which seems to be happening imminently), and usually regret making exceptions to this rule. While I'm on the toilet, Mimi's tail wags furiously at me. I pat her hard pittie head a few times after I finish up, then wash my hands.

Darius calls to Mimi from the front door of our apartment, which is directly across from the narrow bathroom. She immediately scampers the few feet over to him. "Do you want to go for a walk?" he asks her, his low voice rising to a funny pitch as he uses his dog dad voice. I took my shorts off and left them on the bathroom floor and now have on only my crop-top and panties. The panties are high-waisted. They're not lingerie by any stretch of the imagination, but Darius loves them; the sweet, quotidian modesty of them turns him on. Plus, they're 100% cotton, so they let my pussy breathe. As I finish drying my hands, his eyes rake over me, full of heat and knowing— knowing what pleasures await us, knowing that I will be putty in his hands shortly. "I don't want anything interrupting us," he says as he clips Mimi's leash to her harness, all traces of his silly dad dog voice gone and replaced by something deliciously dark. He promptly slips out the door.

I head to the kitchen, deciding it's a good time to unload the dishwasher, while Darius is walking the dog. As I grab the final couple of mugs from the machine's top rack, I hear the heavy wooden door to our apartment close loudly as always, a quirk of living in a building that is over 100 years old. My heartbeat picks up speed in anticipation of what I know is coming next. I hear the bathroom sink going again— Darius washing his hands— as I take my time arranging the mugs, shutting the cabinet, and finally, closing the dishwasher.

I cross our little apartment and stand in the doorway of our room, leaning into the doorframe. Darius is on top of our swirly teal and white comforter— already completely naked— and gripping his hard cock in his hand.

"You don't waste any time, do you?" I say, without moving from my spot at the entrance to our room.

"No, but you do. Bring that ass over here," he commands.

His stern tone just makes me want to rebel more. I turn my body to the side and shift so my ass rests against one edge of the doorframe, grabbing the other side with my hands, arching my back to exaggerate my profile. "This ass?"

Darius strokes his length slowly, the heat of his gaze melting me. "Fine, stay there. I guess you don't want this fat cock."

"No, of course I do!" I whine. I saunter over to our bed and straddle him.

He smiles up at me, smug. "That's what I thought."

I bend over him so we are face to face. In this position, my long curls enshroud us like a curtain.

I rest one fist in the pillow beside his head, and place my other hand on his cheek, which is covered in soft, bushy beard. I graze my smaller nose on his, prominent and strong, gorgeous. As I rub my nose against his, I breathe in his sweet breath, our lips barely brushing against each other. He bounces his hips beneath me and growls impatiently, his hard length against my panties.

"Your breath always smells so good," I say, ignoring his impatience.

"Kiss me," he says, his breath quickening. Teasing him is as much a tease for myself at this point, so I give in, his familiar taste welcoming me home. I move my hand from his cheek to cup the back of his neck, and use the other to grip the headboard above him. Kissing him is like swimming in familiar waters, warm currents rushing over and through me as I float and feel the thrill of nature taking its course.

My tongue presses against his in a soft dance of give and take that makes me wet. Small pecks on the lips intersperse our deeper kisses, making a sweet music as little moans loose from within me. I'm a very vocal lover. I can't help it, and I don't want to.

I move my hand away from the headboard and wedge it between us instead, lifting my hips enough to grab his cock as we continue to make out. Darius inhales sharply when I begin to pull at him gently.

"You like that?" I give his upper lip a playful lick.

"Oh, yeah," he answers, his voice low, almost a whisper.

I kiss Darius' neck and move down toward his chest, letting go of my grip on him for a moment. I kiss him all over his furry body, his soft hair tickling my lips and cheeks. I love his body hair so much. It's a lush forest, soft and sweet smelling. I kiss his belly and his thighs, then playfully bite the latter. He wriggles at the sensation of my teeth against his flesh and I peer up at him from between his legs as I reach for his cock again. He looks back at me, and I notice the hunger in his eyes has morphed. He's still hungry, but instead of devouring me now, his dark eyes are begging, begging me to touch him where he needs it most and do what I will.

I'm kneeling between his legs now, my round ass in the air and my breasts against our comforter. I wrap one hand under his tree trunk of a thigh and wrap the other around his cock, noticing a little bit of pre-cum at the tip. My favorite. I lick the length of his cock with my mouth wide and my tongue flat, and when I reach the tip, I wrap my lips around the head, savoring his salty essence. In unison, we groan deliciously. I giggle at the synchrony and get down to the dirty work I love so much, and how I *do* love sucking Darius' cock. He always describes my blow jobs as *powerful,* which also happens to be his favorite descriptor for my ass.

I kiss down the considerable length of his shaft, work my soft kisses back up to his tip. With my lips still pressed to his flesh, I unleash a small stream of spit through my pursed lips so that it spills down his cock, then work the big thing with my hand, spreading my spit over it and repeating my wet kisses. He is rock hard and watching me intently, in perfect suspense of what I'll do next, even though we've danced this way hundreds of times.

My desire to gobble his cock overtakes me, and I slurp it into my mouth, which elicits a sweet moan from Darius. My mouth works in tandem with my hand, which has a light grip at his base, stroking as I work my mouth up and down his length, swirling my tongue around the head with each upstroke.

After a few minutes like this, I slow down and make space in my mouth, shifting to deepthroat him, angling his tip toward the back of my throat, guiding him in as far as I can take it. I love it, but I can't sustain it for very long, so I shift back to the front space of my mouth, wrapping my lips around his girth and letting myself slobber all over him with the excess saliva building up. I'm working hard to pleasure him and loving every moment, so I let loose a moan, my lips vibrating softly against him from the sound.

"Yeah, you like that?" He loves making me talk with my mouth full.

"Mmhmm," I manage.

"What's that? What do you like?"

I try to answer, *I love your cock in my mouth,* but it comes out as wet, garbled nonsense.

"You want me to fuck your face?" He asks, his tone saccharine mock-innocence, as if he were offering to hold my hand at the park.

"Mmhmm," I beg, attempting to nod my head in a way that would be distinguishable from the way it's already bobbing up and down, and not quite succeeding. I slow my motions down to a stop and let my lips rest lightly wrapped around the head of his cock, my mouth loose, waiting to receive him.

Darius grabs a firm yet gentle fistful of my hair and holds me in place while he bucks his hips to thrust into my mouth, his other hand grabbing desperately at the comforter for balance. I manage a peripheral peek at his face and see his thick brows knitted together in heated concentration. His cock slides between my lips, and my lips continue to vibrate softly as I moan into him.

Finally, my jaw is tired and my pussy's craving is overwhelming, so I give him a few taps on his thigh. He gets the signal and stops, letting loose a great sigh. "Fuck. You melt me."

"I know." I give him a big, drooly smile and shift so I'm kneeling upright. I wipe my mouth with the back of my hand without breaking eye contact.

 **5**

Darius Melts

I'm overwhelmed with a delicious combination of bliss and desire. My head is empty of thought, and I love it. I'm all sensation, pleasure, intense focus on Gabby, who now flops onto her back and spreads her legs open for me. I feast my eyes on the treasure trove between her legs. She usually trims a bit and I can tell it's been awhile since she last did, but I don't give a fuck. I dive right in.

I have to hold myself back from devouring her like I really want to. From our time together and many talks about our preferences, I know that she favors teasing above all else, that is, until she can't take it anymore, when the anticipation becomes too much. "Do I taste good?" she asks me as I venture my first few feather-gentle strokes with my tongue. She tastes incredible, and I let her know by nodding and moaning desperately into her folds. "How good?" she presses breathlessly a moment later. I moan longer and louder in response, a mad man pressing my cock into the mattress while I lick mindlessly.

Now she presses more than just her words against me, holding my head and grinding her pussy lightly against my mouth, my mustache mingling with her curly black bush. Her breath quickens and her moans become frenzied. Next thing I know, she's begging. "Fuck me baby, please, please."

I lift my head and we lock eyes. "Where?" I ask. I love making her say it.

And she loves telling me. Without the barest hesitation, she answers, "My pussy. I need to feel your cock inside me. But keep teasing me, please."

"You're trying to kill me," I say, chuckling at her contradiction, begging at once to be fucked and to be denied, to be teased instead. Teasing her is a tease for me, too, and I am ravenous.

I decide to split the difference in my own way to give her everything she's asking for. I push my middle finger inside her. She's so wet, I feel my cock immediately leak a little pre-cum in response. She gasps as I slowly thrust my finger in and out, in and out. I watch her for a moment before I resume my soft, teasing tongue strokes on her clit. Gabby's breathing hard, with intermittent deep breaths. She read somewhere online that deep breaths intensify pleasure because of their relaxing effect. Her moans after the profound inhales are long and low, as if she's concentrating on not letting herself go over the edge just yet.

"Let me ride you," she pants, and I know this means she's ready, she wants to come on my cock, her favorite way to break apart.

I lie back and get comfortable as Gabby sits up and squirts some lube into her hand, warms it up a little with her fingers against her palm, then rubs it up and down my length (a little gasp escapes me) before slathering it on herself. Gabby rests her knees on either side of my hips, holds my cock in place, and shifts so that her familiar weight comes down on me, slipping me in to the hilt with the most delicious squish I have ever known.

When Gabby rides me, she always takes it easy to start, guiding us into a rhythm. While she grooves on me slowly, I watch her, drink her in, a vision, a goddess, my love. I reach up and caress one breast, my other arm resting behind my head. She grabs my hand and pulls it to her face, licks and sucks each finger, finishing off every digit with a sweet kiss at the tip.

Picking up her rhythm now, Gabby leans down over me so she can hump me a little faster, a little harder. She pins my hands with hers, our fingers interlocked on either side of my head, her wild black curls surrounding us in a curtain again as she kisses me teasingly. I love the contrast of her withholding licks against my lips as her weight slams down on me over and over again. "You want me to come all over your fat cock?" She says.

I am putty, I am melting, I am a mess. All I can manage as a response is to nod vigorously as I moan desperately and we make intense eye contact. Gabby's orgasm is powerful. She grabs the back of my neck and moans loud against my lips as I feel her pulse with sweet release. Her face is too close to mine for me to see anything but her eyes, shining with a vulnerability that bores into my soul, her brows steepled in surrender. I see the wave that washed over her receding from the expression on her face, she exhales sharply and giggles, covering my face with kisses. "Mmm. Thank you, baby," she purrs.

"Thank *you*" I insist. She dismounts, takes a drink of water from the mug on her nightstand, and I check in to make sure she wants me to fuck her doggie style. This is the big finish to our usual little sex routine, and I love it.

"Yes, please," she says, assuming the position: on all fours, gorgeous, fat, jiggly ass in the air, head resting to the side on a mountain of our pillows.

I reapply some lube onto my cock and ease into her, thrusting fully in and out slowly a few times to spread the lube and warm her up again. I love how deep it feels fucking her from this angle. She dirty-talk coaches me to orgasm as I pump into her pussy, then we collapse beside each other on our bed, sweaty and panting.

Gabby puts a hand on my chest, our usual compromise when I'm too hot to fully cuddle and she craves post-sex touch.

"How was it for you?" she asks me, like always.

"You transported me to another world," I say, brain addled. "Did you like it?"

"Mmhmm," she hums in confirmation, her fingers gently clutching my chest hair. "Broccoli cheddar soup sound good for dinner?"

"Mmm," I hum in reply, excited.

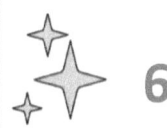

6

Gabby's Woman

What a long, great day. So, why am I lying here at 2 am spiraling?

Of course, Darius fell right to sleep. I always tease him for falling asleep within minutes of going horizontal. Of course, the truth is I'm very jealous of this superpower of his.

He was so open and accepting when I came out to him earlier today. Like he always is. Then why am I feeling like something is different? No, worse— everything is the same but I feel like it *should* be different. It almost feels as if nothing happened at all. Tomorrow, we'll wake up in the same relationship we've been in for seven years. The relationship that has made me so happy, has been everything I've ever wanted.

Of course, nothing about us has changed. We were both bi before coming out to each other. I'm not sure if I've been bi my whole life or if it developed over time. The idea that both nature and nurture worked in tandem to help me come into my sexuality really appeals to me and just feels right, *true.*

Now the self-doubt starts creeping in again. I don't feel any different, so I must not be any different. My own thoughts accuse me: *Am I actually still straight? This thing about being attracted to women and other genders is all a beautiful theory. I'm fetishizing it all because it feels taboo, having been raised Catholic.*

I roll my eyes, jettisoning my next thought of saying a Hail Mary. That always calmed me as a child when I had anxiety at bedtime. It just feels too weird right now, though, as I contemplate my sexuality. It's been years since I've recited a prayer, and admittedly, the people that taught them to me don't usually agree that there's anything to question at all, another part of the heteronormativity-to-violence pipeline I've found myself reflecting on more and more as of late. *Maybe I'm not actually bi, I'm just frustrated with the cis-hetero patriarchy, like all women.*

I try to push back on the self-doubt. *Why am I doing these mental gymnastics?* Following @Poly_Polly on social media has taught me that no one owes anyone "proof" of their queerness. Again, it's something I know in theory, but can't bring myself to feel right now. Instead, I feel confusion. I feel ache. I yearn. My thoughts are like a small horde of bisexual demons at war within me.

You know what you want. Stop lying to yourself. You want to taste her.

Who?

Someone. Someone else. A woman.

Suddenly, homoerotic visions flood my mind, and sapphic yearning pulls at me like a magnet, pulling me toward... what? The unknown.

It's hard to wrap my head around what I'm feeling. Not feeling it for the first time, but acknowledging it for the first time. Maybe naming it for the first time.

Why can't I sleep instead? I don't want to deal with this right now. I'm committed to Darius. We're both bi, yes, but very monogamous.

How did this not come up earlier? Darius isn't one to ask tons of questions. I wonder if he feels this same yearning to be with a man or someone from another part of the gender spectrum.

We were so busy celebrating our intimate vulnerability, sharing in feeling seen, it just didn't come up. Nothing changed. The demons rear their hot heads again.

Nothing has to change! Why does something have to change? I don't need to prove anything.

But if I don't make a woman come, I might die.

I love Darius, but how can I know what my identity even is without experiencing it— reveling in it— fully?

Doubt rushes into my mind and threatens to knock right through my precarious sense of self yet again. *I wouldn't be able to make a woman come. I wouldn't know what to do with her. With myself.* I don't know how to pleasure a woman.

I toss in bed, switching to lay on my other side. I force myself to shove the performance anxiety out of my head with a sharp exhale. With that gone, all I'm left with is desire, profound desire and anxiety at what cannot be. Darius snores softly beside me.

I try to walk back the feeling of impossibleness. How do I know it's impossible? *Aren't threesomes like, every man's fantasy?*

It's like @Poly_Polly always says: *Whatever "It" is, how can you know your partner will or won't be into It until you ask?*

Resolved to engage Darius in yet another tricky yet worthwhile conversation, I finally feel myself drifting toward sleep. I imagine my face buried between some beautiful babe's legs, with Darius behind me, inside me. I hope my dreams in sleep are half this sweet.

7

Vic's Jam

Today is the Barbedbies' first bout of the season, and we're on our home turf. Dee and I ride in together as usual and it's my turn to drive, her lucky silver horseshoe bolo glinting against her chest from her spot in the passenger's seat, under the yellow glow of old streetlights. We warm up as a team, then head to the locker room for Marnie, our coach, to give us a ragey pep talk and pound our strategy into our heads one more time.

After all of this, the locker room fills with the buzzy hum of the team's chatter, everyone shooting the shit until "showtime," which is what we call the moment when we're summoned to the track. I'm on a bench retying my skates when I notice Veronica to my left, fussing at her eye makeup in the mirror on the inside of her locker door. She's usually prickly and full of sassy remarks, but she's quiet and fidgety now. I stand and put my hand on her light brown shoulder, toned and exposed by the uniform tank she's wearing, her derby name, LA LLORONA emblazoned on the back in an arch, as all of ours are.

"Nervous?" I prompt.

She scoffs. "Fucking obviously," she says, turning to face me, causing my grip on her shoulder to release. "I'm gonna get the

45

shit kicked out of me out there."

"Isn't that the point?" I ask, offering her a devious smile.

She smacks her teeth at me and slaps the side of my arm. She sputters, flustered. "Yes, but— Weren't you nervous for your first real bout?"

"Fucking obviously," I say, mimicking her. "I hurled my guts out in the bathroom right before showtime. But I survived, and had a delightful rainbow of bruises as a souvenir, as will you."

Veronica smiles and rolls her eyes. Just then, I hear Marnie's voice ring out again in the locker room: "Showtime, ladies!"

We all echo her in response, a roar of "Showtime!" going up around the room in near-perfect, second-nature unison.

As we skate out of the locker room, Tracy and I exchange a silent nod, the quieter woman matching my pace to stay beside me. On my other side, Rosalind pulls up in a zoom and we do our superstitious tradition of a simultaneous ass-smack, arms windmilling. The piece of pink cloth stretched around her helmet with the green star patch sewn on marks her as our starting jammer. Our quick ritual complete, Rosalind zooms off again to catch up to Veronica, who's at the front of our pack, no doubt to give the rookie her own pep talk.

A couple minutes later, I take my place beside Veronica, bumping my shoulder playfully against hers as I plop down on the lacquered wood bench and size up the team we're facing today, the Ladies of Avon from Morgantown, West Virginia. Our benches are off to the side of the oblong, level track, their team's benches sit across the "O," diagonal from us. If this bout were on a raised track, the benches would be next to each other in the center, coaches and teammates from both teams watching those of us in play go round and round.

Veronica's debut is stunning. She does a great job blocking the other team's jammer once Marnie puts her in, she falls a couple of times and gets up with some help on one fall, then on her own the second time. We beat the Ladies of Avon in a way that probably looks effortless to the small crowd watching. In reality, I attribute our win to the hard sweat and bruises of our preseason practice. We're starting the season off as a well-oiled machine, and I'm beaming with pride.

I don't get much track time today, but I'm okay with it. Marnie's coaching style emphasizes equal opportunity for track time among the team, so I'm confident I will get a chance to dole out (and take) plenty of beatings before the season is over. I knew I wouldn't be in the starting line-up since practice last week, and I don't mind. I'm not the jealous type.

 **8**

Darius and the Proposition

"A threesome?" Blood immediately rushes to my dick. Just saying the words makes me have to adjust myself, sitting at the breakfast table across from Gab. Of course, it's every guy's dream... in theory. It's undeniably, objectively hot. In porn. In mature, happy, enlightened polycules. But not in a seven-year monogamous relationship between two twenty-somethings.

A twinge of jealousy rides in on the wave of horniness. "Wait. Gab, what are you saying? I'm not enough for you?"

"Baby, no. You know that's not what I'm saying. Didn't we just fuck the shit out of each other yesterday? You made me come so hard." She frowns at me.

"That's what I don't understand. Why do you want someone else? Do you feel like you can't be happy without this?"

"No, of course not. But it's something I'd like to explore, so I'm talking about it with you. Think of it more like I want to explore my sexuality, and I want to share that experience with you. I don't want to leave you behind on this adventure. I want you exploring something new right there with me."

"You certainly have a way of twisting words to make them work for you."

"I am a poet, after all." Her playful eyebrow waggle is enough to calm my nervous heart. "But seriously, Darius. Think about it. I know about an app we can download. We can upload a profile, just look, just chat, get comfortable with the idea and keep the conversation open about it. *Then* make a decision."

Panic clutches the heart pounding in my chest as if the feeling is made of strong, spindly fingers. "It sounds like your mind is already made up. You're scaring me a little bit, babe. This feels like it's happening fast."

"Nothing is happening," Gab protests. "We're just talking. I just want to be honest with you. I'd be lying if I said it isn't something that I want. But if you aren't one-hundred percent in, I'll leave it alone. Just promise me you'll think about it, that you'll really consider it."

"Okay. I'll think about it, I guess. It's too early for this shit." I have no idea how I'm supposed to think about anything else at work all day. "I have to catch my bus."

Gabby nods and looks like she might cry. Her big, brown eyes look at me searching for answers, reflecting back more questions and a burden I didn't expect to find waiting for me there. I don't know why I feel heavy looking into her eyes, leaning in for a kiss, but I do. I puzzle over this heavy feeling as I pull away from Gabby and realize the weight is the knowledge that something between us has changed, maybe even something fundamental: that she wants something, badly, and I'm not yet sure if I can give it to her. It's the burden of decision, of selflessness and unwavering responsibility to do right by the woman I love, to honor our commitment to each other.

I don't feel that I have to *have* a threesome. I know she would never force the issue. It's that I feel obligated to consider it, simply because I know if I had suggested something similar, she would consider it for me.

I slip my sneakers on quick by our apartment door. "Love you," I mutter.

"Love you too, baby. Have a great day." Gabby rushes into our room to finish getting ready for her own workday as I step through our front door and into our apartment floor hallway. She's always running late. I shake my head as the door closes behind me, a little smile tugging at the corners of my mouth despite myself as I hustle to make it to my bus on time. All her little quirks endear me.

It's a cloudy day over my bus stop on Wightman Street. *Threesome:* I toss the word up in my head and catch it like a ball. As with questioning our sexualities, it's not like it hasn't come up before. Sometimes we talk about it in bed and it gets us both off, the idea of sharing our hot sex with someone else. But that was all dirty-talk in the heat of the moment, set-dressing, just ambience, like how we watch porn together in bed sometimes. This is totally different. We're talking about flesh-on-flesh *reality*. It *feels* different. And I feel really unsure.

Yes, it's hot in theory, but I worry it could drive a wedge between us. I don't know if I could watch Gabby fuck someone else and be okay with it. Or maybe I'd be okay during, in horny mode, but then a month later, I'd freak out about it. It's completely uncharted territory, and I don't know if I'm ready to explore out there in the real world, exposed.

At the same time, I trust Gabby, and I know she's not going anywhere. And I'm not going anywhere. We're committed to each other. Sexual experimentation is part of what makes life so sweet, and our experiments up to this point have all been rewarded with a deeper understanding of each other and an expansion of our pleasure. We're two people in love, after all, and we don't have anything stopping us but ourselves. If I could just get out of my head about it, maybe it could actually be fun. Or maybe it would ruin us.

Walking into the bakery, I come slightly out of my spiral-stupor when I realize I'm a few minutes late, glancing up at the clock that hangs above the bakery counter. It's a shiny, atomic mid-century thing with long brass spikes, the crowning jewel to the lovingly refurbished, authentic vintage bakery counter. The dusty pink counter frames the chrome refrigeration case, which is already full of fresh pastries Rebecca put out this morning during the early shift.

I swoop into my routine without thinking; it's second-nature for me after four years here at Buttercream, the premier bakery of Pittsburgh's Strip District. The bakery is Dani's family business. She grew up here filling cannolis and watching her grandparents and parents pipe meticulous designs onto countless cakes. Without children of her own, when the torch of business operations was passed to her, she decided to take a different route building her crew. She doesn't call us family or treat us like family. She treats us like employees and even friends because we have a good rapport together, but she doesn't shove any of that toxic "we're all family here" shit down our throats. She treats us well enough that she doesn't have to manipulate us with over-familiar, trite platitudes.

Dani is a great boss with amazing business sense. Some of the other bakeries in town— hell, across the country— pay shit wages and don't bother with benefits, but Dani doesn't run her business like that. She knows what it takes to attract and keep good people, and she has been committed to making Buttercream a great place to work since before Rebecca or I even started. Not only do we have health insurance, paid time off, and 401ks, she also does her genuine best to make Buttercream a dream workplace. Hell, she even took the time to outfit the bathroom into a spa-like experience complete with rainforest-style shower because at different points, at least one of us has been in a gym rat phase and it is so convenient to work out in the gym across the street pre-dawn and shower before the start of a shift. Okay, maybe it also had something to do with wanting to be able to freshen up to the fullest extent after Dani's done getting covered in various sticky confections throughout the day. The shower is wildly luxurious, but I guess I shouldn't be surprised that someone who has made such beautiful, ornate, technically sound delicacies for her entire life applies similar aesthetic principles in other parts of her life and business.

Dani is talented, too. She's away for the next few months being featured on some fancy competitive baking show, and she trusted Rebecca and me to hold down the fort during our busiest season— wedding season— with some seasonal staff to help us with the wedding cakes and cookies for cookie tables, a Pittsburgh wedding tradition.

As I move through the motions of my morning duties, all I can think about is Gabby's proposition. I assemble and decorate yesterday's sponge into cakes, smearing them with the bakery's namesake and icing them with steady hands while my mind feels anything but steady: *Happy Birthday so-and-so; meticulous inside joke; Over the Hill; Taylor Swift lyric;* I pipe the words on the tops of my cakes perfectly, hardly aware of what my calligraphic icing actually says, but making no mistakes.

When the most recent batch of Rebecca's cannoli filling stops spinning, I set myself to filling the shells she made while I was decorating cakes. At the moment, she's up front handing off one of those very cakes to its intended customer. Even from where I am in the back, equipment and ovens and fans humming, I hear happy squeals of approval from the person seeing the cake for the first time. I smile softly and shake my head, picking up another cannoli shell and watching the filling push through from one side to the middle, then turning it and filling the other side. My thoughts swirl toward Gabby again and the cannoli in my hand suddenly becomes a sexual object, its phallic shape impossible to ignore, the filling so creamy and soft...

"Did you catch all that gushing? Nice handiwork," Rebecca says, sauntering into our work area from the back. She startles me, but I am able to suppress the flinch.

I continue moving through cannolis, flicking my gaze up to her face only briefly. "I didn't hear specifics, but I got the gist that she didn't hate it," I say, shrugging one shoulder in an attempt at modesty.

Rebecca doesn't fall for it, though. "Oh, save the humble act for someone who doesn't know you, Darius!" She forms the words around a playful smile, and I smile softly in turn, but I know the smile doesn't reach my eyes as I glance up at her again, setting the cannoli I just filled down on the tray in front of me.

In Rebecca's own eyes, I can see her notice there's something off about me today, but she spares me from any speculating or prying commentary. After four years working together, she knows that I largely keep to myself, that I don't usually like "talking about my feelings" with anyone but Gabby. Whenever there is something I want to get off my chest, if I want to confide in her, Rebecca knows I'll come to her in my own time. We've had some heart-to-hearts over the years, but I can count them all on one hand. Still, the number of people outside my family I trust in this world is small, and I'm grateful to have Rebecca—and Dani—numbering among them.

I genuinely love my job. I fell in love with pastries and cakes in culinary school, and I'm glad I don't have to sacrifice my paycheck for my passion.

 **9**

Gabby's Hatred

I hate my fucking job. My everyday experience is a brain-breaking combination of high pressure, boredom, and I-don't-know-what-the-fuck-I'm-doing.

I'm a legal writer for a law firm that specializes in corporate immigration. I was really excited to work to help folks get and keep their visas, until I realized all the companies who are our clients are complete pieces of shit, evil companies who made this country into the abomination it is today. Well, I guess it was always an abomination, but when I talk about the shittyness of our clients, I'm referring to their role in this late-stage capitalist hellscape in particular. I should have known when I visited the New York office two months ago, when they first hired me, to meet the lawyers I'd be working for. I should have known when I walked past the giant brass bull in the financial district to get to my orientation. But hey, I had gotten a free trip to New York and everyone I met at the home office seemed really nice.

They *were* nice. That wasn't the problem. They simply didn't train me for this job. One day in the office with them flying through five PowerPoint printouts wasn't enough training for me to even begin to grasp what I should be doing as a legal writer. By the end of my eight-hour visit to the New York office, I'd barely grasped the difference between an O-1 and an F-1 visa. That, along with a few dense training videos I have yet to fully make it through, were the full extent of my training for this job. This gig has also subverted my expectation that it would actually be *writerly*. In a way, it's a blessing that it's not. Good writing notoriously depends on the author's basic understanding of their subject matter, at bare minimum. It turns out my job relies almost entirely on templates, so if I could just wrap my head around what the fuck I'm supposed to be doing, I could follow those templates for most of my assignments. My only saving grace so far has been that they're starting me off slow, with plenty of lead time before deadlines.

It's also more than a little strange being required to come into the office every day, but not having any of my supervisors— the lawyers I work for— in the same city as me. They set this office up here in Pittsburgh, initially as their IT center. Then, someone had the bright idea to make it a big writing center as well, with legal writers working for the New York and Chicago offices, the main motivation for the long-distance relationship being that everything is cheaper in Pittsburgh: the building we work in, our salaries. Because $40k in Pittsburgh is livable (for now), when Lily told me I could make that much here, I jumped at the chance to leave my job as an editorial assistant for an economics journal.

Lily and I had worked together at that very economics journal, and she was kind enough to recommend me for the job here at Peterson. They are taking a chance on me because my master's degree is in creative writing, and I sold myself in the interview with my attention to detail and insistence that the expertise afforded to me by my degree is extremely flexible. Plus, my writing sample certainly didn't hurt. They allowed me to submit an academic paper from my undergrad years, and it's one that I'm always impressed with whenever I pull it out of my dusty old computer files.

Yes, I can write, and immigration is an issue that I care deeply about. And the money is enough to pay my rent and my credit card debt, with a little left over to save. *But* I have no idea what I'm doing and no one to help me figure it all out, plus each assignment is more awful than the next. Some jerk who saved a credit card company from going under. Another one who works for some asshole consulting firm. And I'm supposed to make them seem like indispensable, stand-up citizens of society in the fill-in-the-blank templates I'm supposed to be drafting for them.

It's not the immigration part that bothers me, of course. It's the fact that it's *my job* to sing their praises, and that ultimately, what I do is in service to these evil companies. It's also the fact that there's no one here to guide me through the basics of this job, save for those few confusing information-dense videos on the Peterson intranet.

At least there's cake once a month to celebrate all the office birthdays. At least Darius will be happy to see me when I get home.

I click on my email app on my work desktop and open one that seems to be of mild importance. I leave it open so I look busy if anyone passes by my cubicle, and I open my notebook to do some journaling. This isn't the first time I've been stuck in a job I hate, and when I find myself back in this mental state, journaling my internal spirals is the only thing that keeps my head on somewhat straight (or bisexual, more accurately).

I open to a fresh page and try to make sense of it all without judging myself too much. Some of it I feel like I've written a million times before: the stress of a shitty job, the more general stress of living under capitalism, questioning what I even went to school for and whether my degree is worthless, being thankful I had a scholarship.

But there is something new in my journaling today, too. The confession yesterday at the park. The tense discussion with Darius this morning. I don't know how the threesome conversation will turn out, but the feeling of possibility overwhelms me with excitement. It's something to latch onto, it's a puzzle that feels within my capacity to figure out.

Before I know it, it's lunch time and I've managed to procrastinate to the point of accomplishing nothing so far today. I don't care.

I grab my lunch box and head out to my car, where I've been eating lunch and napping to get a bit of outside time, far away from my cubicle. The danger of doing this, of course, though, is the temptation to leave. Every day, I have to fight the urge to walk out into the sunlight, start my car, and never come back. I consider it on every lunch break now, and I know I won't last much longer at this place.

On the drive home, I try to forget the shitty day, the shittier job. I call my best friend Sophie to vent and talk about nothing, what we call "eating shit" back home in Miami: doing nothing important together, even at more than 500 miles apart.

Sophie is my oldest friend. We met when I was in fifth grade and she was in fourth, in a combined class for smartypants rugrats. Looking back, I don't know that I agree with Florida's public school system separating us and our peers like that as part of the "gifted" program, but it brought us together, and for that I am grateful.

We were separated when I went off to middle school, but found ourselves in the same gym class at the same high school years later. More specifically, it was volleyball class, apparently another triumph of the Florida public school system. On the first day, I saw her looking bored with her chin in her hand, elbow resting on her knee as she sat on a bleacher above where I sat in the gymnasium. I called out to her, shouting across the steep expanse of bleachers, "I know you!" She locked eyes with me and the rest is history.

What I miss most about living in the same city as Sophie is running errands together. When we were both living in Miami as young adults before heading off to grad school, I would accompany her to the post office or hang out in her room as she cleaned out a cluttered closet (and leave her place with random odds and ends I'd decided suited me). She would tag along with me on trips to the grocery store or to buy another friend a birthday card. We'd stop for a treat before or after or in between tasks. Sophie's presence made taking care of daunting and menial tasks less so.

When we're together, we talk almost non-stop, braiding threads of conversation that loop over and back on each other. There is always more catching up to do. Nowadays, our reunions are rare and precious occasions. We typically spend those weekends eating and drinking well and shaking our asses out on a dance floor together, greedy to enjoy every moment as much as possible while in each other's presence. We take turns visiting each other, and she never tires of trying to convince me to move to Boston, where she now lives.

Outside, Pittsburgh's signature grey clouds hang over my head as I walk to my car. As soon as I sit in the driver's seat, I station my phone in its holder on the dashboard, unlock it, and click on Sophie's name on my list of recently called contacts. As I pull out of my parking space, I want to roll down my window, unleash a few screaming expletives, and stick my middle finger up at the place I hate most in the world.

The phone rings over my car speakers and tears blur the red traffic light as I wait to turn onto McKnight Road, which will bear me most of the way home.

Just as I'm starting to think I've missed her, anticipating her outgoing voicemail message, Sophie picks up. She answers the phone with her classic "Hellooo" in the overdone Miami accent we love to play up.

I can't help but chuckle. I wipe the tears from my eyes as I press on the gas. "Hey."

"How are you, bud? Are you okay? You didn't return my 'hellooo.'" Concern tinges her words.

"No, I'm not great. Do you have a bit? I'm driving home from hell right now."

"Yeah, no worries. I just got home. What's up? Talk to me." I can easily imagine the look on her face, almost see her eyes widening, with worry, yes, but also receptive, showing me she's ready to listen.

Sophie is a great listener, and she never makes me or my problems feel small. She is my favorite shoulder to cry on, though of course since she lives in Boston now, we do our shoulder-crying virtually most of the time these days.

I sigh, and it feels like my zillionth exhausted sigh of the day. "I don't know how much longer I can do this. This fucking job is killing me. I'm not trying to be dramatic, but it's just not what I envisioned for myself. And you know how I am with my anxiety. So naturally I feel like I'm wasting the only life I've got in this cubicle, and not even for a good cause. The clients for this law firm are fucking evil, dude."

Sophie makes a soft, sympathetic clucking sound. "Aw, that sucks, bud. I'm sorry. Have you been applying to other stuff?"

"I don't even know what kinds of jobs I should be applying to." My voice comes out higher-pitched and whinier than I intend it to, but I feel a leaden wave bearing down on me as I let myself unleash my honest feelings. "Even though the pay was shit, I regret leaving my editorial assistant job and I feel like there aren't that many of those here in Pittsburgh. Turns out I hate being a legal writer. I don't want to be a professor— not that I could even land a decent adjunct gig if I tried. I feel like my master's degree is worthless." The admission leaves me with a hollow feeling in my chest, but I let the momentum of my blathering carry me to finish my cathartic tirade. "It's not like I have the energy to be creative right now. I'm not even writing, I don't feel like myself. I'm scared I'll forget how to write poetry at all. What was all that work for, going to grad school? I feel like I fucked up my life." I'm out of breath. My next inhale is sharp and followed by another heavy sigh.

"That's a lot to carry. You've got a lot of things swirling around right now," Sophie says.

"I just want to quit." I'm at another stoplight, so I take a moment to lean my forehead against my steering wheel, feeling awash in hopelessness.

"I know, Gabs, and I support you, but you'll feel so much better if you pay off your credit card debt and line something up first. Remember, that was your big goal. Then, you can move onto something else. Anything. Maybe you could just get whatever job, something temporary to pay the bills. Just to get out of there and figure out your next move."

"Retail?" I feel my voice crack as the tightness returns to my throat.

"It may not be ideal, but if you're this miserable... I don't know, bud. I'm just trying to help you think about potential scenarios you might find yourself in. Solutions, if you will. Potential— albeit not perfect— solutions."

I sigh again. With the distance growing between me and the office, the weight feels lighter. It already feels far away, which makes the situation feel manageable all of a sudden. "Maybe it's not so bad," I consider aloud. "Maybe I'll get the hang of it."

Sophie hums in agreement. "You know I believe in you, Gabs. If you put your mind to it, you can do it. I know it's hard. I know it sucks and they didn't train you well."

"Yeah," I agree. "It's hard to remember if anything else has been this hard before."

"You've had a lot of jobs, bud!" Sophie chuckles. "Are you sure this is even the worst?"

"I know," I admit, smiling and rolling my eyes at my own busy, scattered past. Things have been complicated. The longest I've ever stayed at any job was a little under two years, and it was my very first job as a senior in high school. I consider the scattered mosaic of jobs I've had since them, each one flashing briefly before my mind's eye. "Yeah, you're right. They've all pretty much sucked."

Sophie gives me a few more updates on how things are going with her. Her new job doesn't pay her what she deserves, but she figures she has to stay there for at least a year to build the credibility she needs for her next step. She's an occupational therapist. It's a job I don't fully understand in a day-to-day way (I know, shocking from someone like me who has such a firm grasp on her own occupation), but I get the broad strokes, and that seems to be enough.

When I pull into my parking spot at my apartment building, Sophie is telling me about some of the drama in her new rock climbing friend group. As she talks, I reflect on how Sophie is blending into her niche of New England life seamlessly now. It would seem effortless to any outsider, but I know how much she went through to build a life there. It isn't easy to make friends as an adult, much less in a new city.

Of course, new cities lend themselves to new experiences, but finding footing in uncertain territory can feel treacherous, especially when it comes to making friends. Sophie surmounted all of that and is thriving now, though. In her element. It's fitting that she has grown to love— and excel at— rock climbing.

She finishes her story and I turn off my car. "I have to run in a sec, but I actually do have something fun to share," I say.

"Ooooh," Sophie coos in a sing-song.

"Well, recently I figured out I'm bi—" I start.

Sophie interrupts me with a squeal of excitement. "Congratulations, Gabs! I'm not surprised but I'm very stoked for you and your journey," she says. "Welcome to the club!" She cackles at this last cheesy remark.

I chuckle. "Thank you, thank you. Happy to be here. Of course, after coming out to Darius yesterday, I was up half the night spiraling."

"Of course," Sophie echoes, understanding, but not agreeing.

"So this morning, I brought up the possibility of maybe he and I... having a threesome?" The end of my sentence sounds like a question, like I can't quite bring myself to admit the conversation with Darius this morning was actually real.

Sophie hollers wordlessly, unable to contain her excitement. "Oh my God, what did he say?"

10

Darius Yes-Ands

I'm back on the bus and the déjà vu is heavy on my mind. I haven't sorted through my feelings from Gabby's proposition any more than I had when I rode the bus into work this morning. My workday was a blur. I was distracted, the pendulum of my emotions swinging wildly from concern to jealousy to lust to nonchalance to sadness to excitement. If anything, I have even more questions now. What if I let my dick think for me and everything turns out to be a disaster? Not only am I unsure whether I can handle seeing Gabby fuck someone else, but can she handle seeing me do it? My cock perks up a little despite myself at the excitement of the unknown, but the worry of whether Gabby would be okay in this scenario clouds my mind.

Before long, I'm walking up the wooden ramp of Improv N'at, barely aware of how I arrived here. I have class tonight. In the back of my mind, I wonder idly how many Pittsburgh businesses have "n'at" or "steel" in their names. "N'at" is a yinzer contraction for the words "and" and "that." It basically means "et cetera." Most small businesses here use dashes of Pittsburghese in their branding. Some make it their whole brand. Improv N'at falls somewhere in the middle of this spectrum. They definitely play into the Steel City aesthetics, but their vibe has also been strongly influenced by the New York improv scene.

The owners are a married couple. One of them, the wife, was born and raised in Pittsburgh. She moved to New York City to study acting and singing and musical theater, and fell in love with improv, and her husband (from upstate) while there. Fast forward some years, and she comes back to Pittsburgh, bringing her beau along with her. They marry and conceive of their first child: Improv N'at.

I love many things about improv, not the least of which being that it's fun, and I get to laugh almost non-stop for three hours of class time, once a week. But, it's not just that. Improv has taught me to be present, to react honestly in the moment to the world around me, to the people in my life.

We joke amongst ourselves that improv is a little bit cult-y, especially because we devotees are always very enthusiastic about welcoming new and prospective recruits. I have been a fan of improv, coming to shows at Improv N'at, for years. It's only been about three months of class for me, though. I'm in the second level of the track offered at the theater. At the end of each two-month class, there is a class show. It's exactly what one might imagine, like a recital: a graduation performance.

Improv has definitely helped my creativity, too. It feels so good to play as an adult, to do something just for the fun of it. I feel it at work, my brain entering the same sort of "flow state" when I'm piping a cake as when I'm onstage.

While we do learn new skills some weeks, other sessions are for reinforcing the basics we learned in Level 1. Our instructor, Sean— who has also become my friend since I started coming to shows at Improv N'at— takes a few minutes to go over today's lesson before we dive into scene work. I make a concerted effort to dial back the noise in my brain so that I can lock into what he's saying.

"Let's *really* focus on 'yes, and-ing' our scene partners today," Sean says, his gaze gliding over the risers where we sit, the same chairs occupied by the audience during shows. "Listen closely, actively, then yes-and the absolute crap out of whatever your partner has introduced. Remember to play at the height of your intelligence, think about what you can give to your partner to make them look like a genius onstage."

Yes, and is the fundamental rule of improv, which is by nature a collaborative art. *Yes, and* is all about agreeing with whatever one's scene partner has set forth— not necessarily with what they're saying, but with the universe they've created. That's the *yes* part. The *and* comes in when we add to the scene they've started to spin from thin air, building upon the universe we create together.

Sean's words have stirred something unexpected in me, like he kicked a tiny stone loose, and what comes next is an unstoppable rockslide. I don't *need* to say yes to Gabby's proposition, but I want to, despite my hangups.

I had an idea of what the *and* could be in this scenario while I was at work today, a way to build upon Gabby's idea, but I'd pushed it away before I could let the thought fully form. It might be genius, or it might be foolish, but that, too, is all part of the beauty of the art that is improvisation. I won't know until I initiate the scene with her, I won't know unless I try.

There's a lot more at stake in my relationship than in an improv scene, but for now, focusing on how I might *yes, and* Gabby helps my fear transform into creativity, much like the stage fright I experienced at the start of my improv journey.

As I approach our apartment, I can already hear reggaeton bumping softly against the door, smell something garlicky wafting into the hallway. I enter our living room and everything gets louder— sounds and smells. Mimi gives a brief bark at the sound of my arrival, then runs from the kitchen to greet me before dashing back to be with Gabby. She must always be at Gabby's side.

Gabby herself peeks her head out of the kitchen now, hanging off the doorframe. "Honey! Thank goodness you're home. I missed you!" I smile as I take my shoes off. I swear I'll never get tired of coming home to her welcome. I walk over to the kitchen and take a deep whiff.

"What's cookin', good lookin'? Late-night dinner smells good," I muse at her back, letting my eyes drift down to her ass for the moment before she turns to face me. She's not wearing anything particularly special, just a t-shirt and a pair of unremarkable, sky blue high-waist cotton panties. Still fixated on her lower half, in my periphery, I see that she catches the slant of my gaze immediately. I drag my eyes back up her body until they meet her own, which in this very moment dance with playfulness, but I don't miss the tired haze that clouds them, too.

"See something you like, perv?" she teases.

"If marveling at your perfect ass is wrong, I don't want to be right," I answer, laying a flat, earnest hand on my chest.

She hums in mock-disapproval. "Frozen Mandarin orange chicken and fried rice. I hope that's okay. It'll be ready soon."

"Sounds yummy."

For now, I plant a smooch on her forehead. She often snacks and waits for me to get home so we can eat dinner together on days I have improv class, which ends around 10.

Gabby sighs, leaning her forehead into my kiss. "I had such a horrible day. I fucking hate my job."

"I know, baby, I'm sorry," I say.

"It's okay. I'll get out of there soon. I'm paying off my stupid credit card debt. Trying to keep my eye on the prize. How was your day?" She gives me another kiss and wraps her arms around my waist. The scene is quotidian, but something seems different about her. I can't quite put words to it, but I know it's the same change blooming within my own chest.

I look down at her and give her the same answer I do almost every time she asks me how my day went. "Same shit, different day."

Gabby rolls her eyes. "Do I get anymore details today? Any pretty cake pics?"

"Nah." I shrug.

She lets go of me and turns to mind the chicken and rice on the stove. "I'm sorry about this morning. I didn't mean to spring that on you. You know how I get. I just couldn't sleep last night, I was spiraling about it and I got super fixated. Then I felt like I had to tell you first thing this morning. I didn't want to keep it inside or keep it secret or anything, you know?"

"I understand." I take a deep breath. "Honestly, I haven't stopped thinking about it all day. You really caught me off-guard with this proposition, Gab."

She laughs and mimics me a little. "'Proposition.' So serious."

"I mean, I don't take something like this lightly," I say.

"No, neither do I. But I'm trying to think of it like anything else in our relationship. A conversation. An open dialogue. 'Proposition' makes it sound so formal, kind of scary. To me, anyway." She puts her fingers to her chest for emphasis and they draw my gaze to her gorgeous breasts, which are generously spilling out of the cami she's wearing.

"Okay. Well I *am* glad to hear you say that, because I have something new to contribute to this 'dialogue.'" I throw the silly mimicry right back at her. "I had an idea today." I let my voice drawl on the word *idea,* as if I were dipping it in honey. "Let's eat dinner, then we can talk after."

Gabby raises her eyebrows playfully at me, curious. She looks as if she's about to burst, but she manages to hold her tongue. I think she's possibly been stunned into silence by my cryptic announcement.

After dinner, we decide to shower together, and I finally begin to explain myself. "I want to make a deal with you." I pause for effect, hoping I sound sexy as I watch the warm water pour over her shoulders, tiny droplets bouncing off her skin in every direction. Though maybe I should have, I hadn't expected the prowling sense of anticipation in my guts as I suggest a fantasy tradeoff with my girlfriend. I don't even know if she's going to go for it. I continue, "I know you want to have a threesome, and honestly, I think it would be incredibly hot. But I have a lot of concerns about potential insecurities and weirdness that could come up for us."

Before I can say more, Gabby cuts in, her excitement big as life in her voice. "I know. I agree. I think we should definitely make sure to talk through that sticky stuff— that's what she said— thoroughly." She snorts a laugh, then lets out a whoosh of air in an effort to be more serious. "Sorry. Continue." She gives me a little push so that I can take a turn with the warm water. I shift in the narrow space to swap places with her.

"Anyway, before I was so *rudely* interrupted," I say with bravado, her excitement and silliness contagious. "I was *saying* that in addition to talking through weirdness and setting good boundaries together, I want to make a *deal* with you." Butterflies flutter in my stomach. As if she can sense my nerves, Gabby takes my loofah off of its hook on the pink-tiled shower wall, squirts some of my body wash onto it, and lathers with her hand after wetting it a bit. She scrubs the sudsy loofah gently against my wet chest and shoulders, listening to me speak. The gentle tenderness of the moment has the butterflies stilling, has me breathing deeply to steady my courage.

"I have been doing some thinking at work. Not that I'm always thinking about sex at work." Gabby's eyebrows climb even higher than they had at the start of this conversation, but she waits for me to finish, re-soaping the loofah and resuming her washing of me, now getting to work on my belly. "I want to try food play," I blurt out. Gabby freezes mid-soap swirl and her mouth pops open into a smiling "O." She lets out a surprised huff of air that's almost a giggle. Before she can form whatever this expression means into words, I add, "It's all the buttercream and piping and cannolis and cakes and dough and *sweetness!* I don't know." Gabby crouches silently before me but does not break eye contact with me as she lathers the loofah against my legs, coating my dark leg hair in white suds. "I guess I've always noticed a sensuality to my work, to baking. It's not just that I work with my hands, but I make things that are so indulgent, so *delicate...*" I feel my dick begin to swell a bit, apparently inspired by my own impassioned speech. I shrug and meet Gabby's gaze. "And I have a thing for texture— soft, spongey things, creamy things. Everything I make at work is perfect. I don't care if that sounds arrogant." With both hands, I form my fingers into a pinched shape for emphasis. "I make perfect little delectable creations, and I have this growing hunger to just... destroy them in the most hedonistic ways possible." I spread my pinched fingers in a blasting motion, almost like making jazz hands.

"Okay, now I'm listening," Gabby says. She maneuvers me gently, turning me toward the stream of shower water to rinse the front half of me that she's covered in soft suds. As I obey her subtle cue, I wonder what thoughts are flitting behind her eyes, though in the gaze she casts upon me I can guess at pleasant surprise and mischief. I know her well enough to know she hadn't expected this bargain from me.

I continue. "So, I want to explore my interest in exchange for exploring yours. I want to approach these experiments with good faith, *hoping* to come out of them with new shared interests, but not necessarily expecting to. I definitely think we need to hold space for the possibility that we might not be into the thing the other person is into, at the end of the day. Unless you already hate the idea. Then I suppose we can figure something else out." On these last words, I let my voice balance on a tightrope of teasing and sincerity, because though I would never pressure her, the expression on her face is already telling me that she likes my idea. Even though after all this time it's a given between us, I still know it's worth voicing that her refusal is always an option.

A devilish grin spreads on Gabby's face. "You want to... lick buttercream off my tits?" The loofah she used on me is still covered in suds. With her hand, she scoops some off of the loofah and rubs circles of its woods-scented white fluff on her wet breasts. She hangs the loofah back on its hook and cups her breasts as if in offering to me, biting her lower lip in mock-shyness. "Would it look kind of like this?"

With my right finger, I trace a spiral onto her left breast, inching closer and tighter to her nipple with each circular stroke. "Yeah, and my tongue would feel kind of like this when I lick it off," I answer, swiping my finger in an upward motion, directly across the peak of her nipple, through the spiral I drew.

Gabby hums hungrily in answer and leans her forehead onto my chest, wrapping her arms around my waist, the water coming down around both of us. After a moment, she lifts her head and rests her chin on my sternum, her big brown gaze diving into mine. "You've got yourself a deal. Shall we seal it with a kiss?" I lean down and take her mouth against mine, our tongues meeting tip to tip, tentative, as if exploring the new territory we just opened up between us.

I pull away. "We still have a lot to talk about," I say.

"We have all the time in the world," Gabby replies, then pulls me in for more steam-shrouded kisses.

The next day, I'm practically vibrating on my ride home after work on the bus, almost bursting with excitement to see Gabby, to explore together. As we toweled off last night, we decided we'd do some "research" today into our newly revealed interests, into actualizing this bargain we made. We discussed keeping things light and curious, open-minded.

I am exhausted from working the early shift at the bakery the day after staying up late post-improv class last night. I can't resist a nap (nor do I want to) when I get home, flopping onto the bed after hastily stripping down to my boxers. Drifting off to dreamland, I decide I will make us a simple linguine for dinner.

Gabby's arrival home is announced by the unruly slam of our front door. A few moments later, I feel her slip her arms around me from behind as I mind the cheesy-creamy, herb-flecked sauce on the stove, her splayed hands resting on my chest. "What's cookin' good lookin'?" She asks in a deep voice.

"I do not sound like that," I protest, turning to face her. Gabby studies me, her brown eyes searing me. It's like she's seeing me for the first time in a long time, like I'm a puzzle she wants to not just solve, but luxuriate over, bringing me back together piece by piece. "But, to answer your question," I continue, "we're having a simple linguine tonight, and I can already promise that it's going to be very yummy."

Her voice simmers low and I want to bite the wicked little smile on her lips. "Making yummy promises already?"

I brush a soft kiss against her lips, and inspiration sparks inside me. "I can do more than make promises. What do you think about having dessert before dinner?"

Gabby's smile widens. "Sounds delicious."

I open the fridge and lean down to grab one of our plastic food storage boxes I brought home a couple days ago filled with a half-dozen cannolis. I notice there are only two left in the box now.

"You hardly saved me any," I chastise.

"You can eat as many as you want at work. Whatever you bring home in there is *mine,*" she announces brattily.

I feel the bulge in my boxers grow bigger, heat surging through me. Her bratty tone just awakened the beast in me that had clawed at its cage all day, dreaming of the beautiful messes I want to make with her. My inner beast is ravenous. She grabs the plastic container of cannolis, playing keep-away. She is standing at the counter across the entryway to the kitchen, her back to me. She darts a mischievous glance over her shoulder at me, all eyebrows and eyelashes.

"You better not eat them both," I warn. "If you do, I just might not bring anymore home."

As if an extra in *Kill Bill,* she whirls around on one socked foot at martial-arts speed to face me. "You wouldn't dare," she says low, laying the drama on thick. She squints her eyes at me, pressing me, challenging me.

I close the gap between us, crossing the few paces slowly, letting the room fill with our breathy anticipation, which I sense growing molasses-thick now. Gabby opens the plastic container and sets it down on the counter with the lid beside it, then hoists herself onto the counter perpendicular to them. She kicks her heels lightly against the bottom cabinets, making a soft knocking sound.

Gingerly, I lift a cannoli from the open box and lean into Gabby, between her open legs. Gabby smiles up at me, and I let my hard length graze against her leg, leaning onto the counter with my other hand. Her smile widens. "Tongue out," I command, my voice a growl. She obeys immediately, smile unwavering as she lets her jaw go slack to open her mouth and stick her tongue out, the prettiest shade of pink, her eyes alight with expectation, refusing to break contact with mine. I move the cannoli a hair's breadth from her lips, and, my voice almost a whisper, I say, "Lick."

Gabby cranes her neck to close the short distance to the cannoli, swiping her pretty pink tongue against the creamy filling bursting out the end closest to her. I watch as, after a few licks, she gives the cannoli an open-mouthed kiss, drawing the filling between her lips and into her mouth in a way that makes my cock twitch hungrily. I shift the angle of the cannoli and start in on my end, going for a direct, big bite that I know will destabilize the whole thing. Sure enough, crisp flakes fall onto the shelf of Gabby's glorious breasts, which are mostly on display since she's just in her bra and panties, her clothes no doubt slumped over the arm of the couch in the other room.

Gabby reacts quickly, trying to grab onto the cannoli along with me in an attempt to keep it together, but it's too late. We're both holding a crumbling mess with ricotta-based filling bursting at the seams. "Let go," I say, but Gabby hesitates.

"It's going to fall everywhere!" Gabby squeals.

"Let go," I repeat, too wrapped up to explain myself further or engage in any kind of banter right now. Gabby releases her hold on the cannoli and I take what is left and crush it in my hand to finish breaking the tunnel-like shell. The creamy filling oozes on either side of my fist and between my fingers, a thick dollop landing on Gabby's left breast.

I spread my hand in a sort of playful warning and Gabby understands my intention a split-second before I act. She gives a delightful squeal like she's being tickled and before she's out of breath, my hand is all over her breasts, spreading the cannoli mess all over them. We laugh and I feed her bits of shell heaped with filling, she swipes her finger on herself and feeds me globs of the stuff.

After a minute, Gabby says, "No fair, I barely got any. All of it ended up on my tits." She gives me a pout, then nudges me back with her legs and slips from the counter down to her knees. She hooks her fingers into the elastic and pulls my briefs down, my hard cock seeming almost to jump out eagerly at her with the motion. She grabs it firmly but gently and, sitting as tall as she can on her knees, she arches toward me and rubs her messy tits all over my cock, now mostly just filling and the occasional mini chocolate chip.

"You're making such a mess," I chastise softly, but I'm barely able to get the last word out because she's licking me from my base to the head of my cock, and now her sweet lips are wrapped around the tip, giving it the same open-mouth kiss I watched her use on the cannoli moments ago. She licks and kisses my entire length methodically, voraciously, cleaning me up in earnest.

Once she's cleaned me up and made my cock very slick on all sides in the process, she wraps her lips around the head and slowly, agonizingly slowly, slips her mouth down its length until my tip grazes the back of her throat. We're still close enough that I'm able to lean on the counter behind her and right now I feel like I need to because what Gabby is doing to me has my knees feeling jelly-filled.

After the sweetest blowjob of my life, we clean ourselves up and shower, then eat our linguine (indeed simple, but delicious). I take the dishes to the sink in the kitchen. As I finish rinsing the last plate and sliding it into a slot in the dishwasher, I call out to Gabby, who is sitting on the couch. "Are you ready to do some research?"

"I was born ready, baby," Gabby half-shouts from the other room. Then, she adds in a sing-song voice, "But I think the research has already begun!"

I close the faucet and dry my hands on the tea towel that's been hanging from our oven door handle for too long, making a mental note to just change the damn thing already, soon. Soon, but not now. Now is the time for research. I stalk to the living room.

A sighing groan looses itself from my throat as I throw myself into the sinking couch cushion that is my de-facto assigned half of the couch. I pull out my phone. "Ready? I want to show you something."

Gabby's eyebrows wriggle playfully, dancing above her smiling eyes, her lips looking like they might burst into giggles at any moment. She takes a steadying breath and leans into me, the side of her head resting on my upper arm, the soft part below my shoulder.

Gabby watches as, with a few swift thumb-strokes, I pull up Food Freaxxx on my phone's browser. I log in. "Oh my God, you already have an *account?*" On the last word, the tone of her voice lifts in surprise, but it's not an accusation.

I nod, my excitement growing. "I just made it earlier today. I didn't even know such a thing existed until I started doing some poking around online. I thought we could maybe actually interact with some of the other people on here in a way to... *feed* the fantasy. Both of our fantasies." I smirk.

"I see what you did there," Gabby sings. "You know I love a good pun!" Then, she bites her bottom lip as her gaze locks on the first image in the feed now on my screen. It's a rock-hard cock with a dollop of whipped cream on the tip, a video. Gabby reaches over me and presses play.

11

Gabby and Carmen

After only an hour scrolling through the FoodFreaxxx "feed" (perfectly apt, I know) where a small community posts their latest homemade food fetish content, I am starting to get what Darius was driving after with his half of the bargain. Some of these posts are wildly hot. The little bit of fabric that forms the central panel of my panties is already soaked, my thighs pressed together in need.

After watching a five-second loop of someone fucking themselves with a red lollipop for the tenth time, Darius scrolls to the next post. I press my hand to the hardness between Darius' legs as the next video starts up, my curiosity turned to a craving that is becoming overwhelming. On the screen is a beautiful woman with fiery, thick red curls splayed out on a purple blanket around her as she looks up at the camera. I notice that her username is @ViciousVulva and this makes me instantly like her.

As we watch, @ViciousVulva hypnotizes us by rubbing little ice cream sandwiches all over her perfect tits, then licking off the mess, pausing to indulge in eating the cookies themselves throughout. I feel my breath coming harder, heat flushing my cheeks as well as my core. Darius lets out a soft moan, and I realize my teasing, absent-minded toying with his cock has turned into me stroking him with an intense rhythm and grip. I don't know when I started jerking him off in earnest over his soft briefs, but my need for him is turning all-consuming now.

Most of the videos on Food Freaxxx are short, and this one is only two minutes long. "Restart it," I tell Darius in a low voice, almost a whisper, my breaths becoming increasingly ragged. Without saying a word, he obeys, and I reposition myself on the couch so that I'm on all fours, facing him. As he watches the video, I free his hard cock from his briefs with one hand, pulling down at the waistband, then lick it on either side before sucking him down.

"You like watching her, baby?" I ask after a few bobs up and down his length.

"Mmhmm," he says, and I can tell it's all he can manage right now, brows knitted together to frame his wide-eyed desire, as if it's all just too much for him and he's overwhelmed with his own need.

I give his cock another playful lick and keep pumping it as I say, "Me, too. Tell her how much we like watching her. Let's leave her a nice comment for putting on such a spectacular show for us." I dive back down onto him, mouth first.

"I've got it," Darius announces almost right away, even with the distraction of me not letting up on him in the slightest. Darius reads his comment aloud. "Incredible. Wish you could be the cream in the middle of our sandwich."

One of the other things we did in the last hour was put together a hasty couple's profile, including what I now think is a series of too-wholesome profile pictures, so she'll know exactly who the two cookies are who want her in the middle of "our" sandwich: It's these two dweebs on vacation, in Miami in some photos, New York in others, squinting in the sun but beach-kissed and happy here, exploring the big city doing all the stereotypical tourist things there.

I yank my mouth away from Darius' length, but I keep my mouth in an "O" formation to match my surprise and delight at his witty-sexy-flirty comment. "Babe," I squeal. "Those improv classes are really paying off!" He rolls his eyes at me and I giggle before bobbing my head back down, fitting my lips around him and sliding down until I feel his tip hit the back of my throat.

"I'm feeling inspired," I tell Darius as we're toweling off together in our pink-tiled bathroom after our post-romp shower.

"Me too," he purrs. "Who wouldn't feel inspired after that?"

I smirk at him. "I'm doing it. Fuck it. I'm applying for some retail jobs tonight, I don't care. I'll apply to that trendy grocery store— the people there seem nice and happy."

"Go for it, babe. I support you. You're miserable at that fuckin' law firm. I don't care what you do, as long as you're happy and you can still pay half the rent." Now it's my turn to roll my eyes at him. I take my brattiness a step further and snap my towel at him halfheartedly, nothing that could actually hurt him. He yelps, then says, "I'm sorry, I wish I were a rich man, but I'm not!"

"Excuses, excuses," I tease. I hang my towel up. Darius has his wrapped around his waist, and the feel of its damp cotton is not unpleasant against my bare skin as I lean against him and take a deep breath, my chin resting in the humid curls on his chest as I look up into his big, dark eyes. "Thank you for being so supportive," I say, letting my tone weigh with sincerity now.

He pops a sweet kiss onto my lips. "You don't have to thank me, Gab. I love you and I'll support you no matter what. I don't care what you do for work. I just want to be with you." At that, I feel my eyes prickle. Now it's my turn to pop a kiss on his lips.

I get into one of my usual, at-home-and-comfy crop tops and head to the grocery store website. It takes me 30 minutes to apply to the location closest to us, zinging cover letter and all.

A week after submitting my application, I'm sitting in my cubicle when I get a call from a number I don't recognize. It has a 412 area code, so I know it's local. I practically sprint to one of the quiet booths that are probably intended for phone calls way above the pay grade of anyone who actually works in this building. I try not to sound out of breath as I answer the phone. "This is Gabby," I say.

An energetic, deep voice answers on the other line without hesitation. "Hi Gabby, this is Max. We got your grocer application and would like to invite you in for an interview. When are you available?"

I try not to squeal in excitement. I don't want to jump the gun, but my brain is already chanting, *I'm free, I'm free, I'm freeeee!* After a little bit of schedule wrangling, we nail down a date and time for the interview. Actually, it turns out that if I do well interviewing with two assistant-managers, they'll have me meet with the store general manager right away that same day. "I look forward to meeting all of you," I chirp in my best customer-service voice, and do a little happy dance as soon as I hang up.

A week after that phone call, I leave the store with a job offer made by them and accepted by me on the spot. As I try not to get run over in the chaos of driving customers while walking back to my car, I could almost swear the parking lot pavement is glittering with dreams fulfilled. I feel like maybe I'm in a musical and the song in my heart might burst out of my mouth at any moment and the entire city of Pittsburgh would join me in perfect harmony and choreography because... *I can quit my shitty cubicle job!* Though I won't be able to afford my fancy manicures anymore, I'll be *free*.

It's an odd feeling to wake up with a smile on my face, literally. I feel like when I get out of bed, I might levitate to the kitchen to make my coffee. Today is the day I get to quit and fuck all the way off. I will collect my few belongings, the scraps of myself that brought me joy in that grey cubicle, and then I will get to leave forever and move on with my life.

I decide to forego the use of my espresso machine in favor of making Cuban coffee the old fashioned way. I fill the chamber with water and assemble my cafetera, my stove-top espresso maker. After putting the cafetera on stove heat, lid open, I scoop sugar into the household measuring cup and wait for the first spurt of coffee to trickle-jump out of the cafetera's inner spout. While I wait, I pour myself some milk, then heat the mug of it in the microwave.

Soon, the awaited first nip of coffee is released from the spout, having pushed its way up through the pinhole-sized filters. I shut the lid and grab the cafetera, then gently tilt it toward the measuring cup until a few drops spill onto the sugar. Knowing how much coffee to add to the sugar is an art, and I don't get it right on the first time every try. Sometimes I end up having to add more sugar to perfect the ratio for the proper consistency.

This morning, the first time is the charm. I set the cafetera back onto the stove so the coffee can finish brewing, and while it does, I swirl the sugar and bit of coffee vigorously. This is the trick to the espumita, the foam, of Cuban coffee. When served alone, it floats at the top of the tazita, light brown in contrast with the almost black color of the rest of the espresso shot. This effect is lost with café con leche, coffee with milk, which I have my heart set on this morning. Still, the hint of sweetness will finish off the café con leche's flavor profile perfectly.

Café con leche is the breakfast beverage I grew up with. It's what I have every day, whether I make Cuban coffee for it or make a regular at-home latte version of it with the espresso machine.

I make some toast, then sit with my breakfast on the couch, precariously balancing the mug on the same plate my toast sits on. I dip the toast in my morning coffee, a childhood tradition whose nostalgia warms my whole body. Longing gives me a bittersweet smile. I sigh, then reach for my laptop on the coffee table in front of me.

It doesn't take me more than ten minutes to type the email, read it over, and send it. It would have only taken me five, but the nerves made me read it and reread it and read it a final time, aloud. Truly, it doesn't matter much what it says. It looks bad that I'm quitting, no matter how I put it. I might as well have just sent the words, "I quit." It's not like I can depend on them for a reference. I had barely done any work for them. The work I had done was turned in late. I had absolutely no clue what I was doing and a desire to learn that dwindled as I unraveled more about each client.

Now sent, I release another sigh, this one sharp as I push the air out of me in an attempt to feel some kind of finality. Our cat, Groovy, jumps onto the arm rest of the couch just to my left, as if to come check on me. Mimi is asleep on the other side of the couch already, on her own dedicated pillow.

I guess it's just luck that the sun is shining so brightly and the sky is clear, blue. I am ecstatic. Today, my fantasy of driving off the Peterson lot, erased by sunshine, comes true.

I put on a hyperpop playlist and try not to speed too much on my way to pick up my office plants and gossip about myself. While driving, I imagine their reactions. Ella at the front desk will probably say something like, "I can't believe you're leaving before me!" I hope one of my last acts as a Peterson employee is becoming her confidant. She seems so cool. Hopefully Lily won't be too annoyed at me and we can still stay in touch.

That night, Darius and I eat the dinner he made as he listens intently to my recounting of how it went at Peterson, how surreal it was leaving for the last time. Ella and I did exchange numbers, so I'm hopeful I made a new friend. Lily seemed unruffled; I don't think she's worried that my departure will affect her standing in any way for having recommended me. I cried on the drive home, the wind in my hair as I hollered along with my playlist blaring through the car stereo.

Then, we cuddle on the couch and watch a few episodes of an anime that he loved as a kid. We started watching it a couple weeks ago, and it really holds up. It's beautiful to watch, and it's beautiful to know a piece of art that shaped him into the person he is today. It gives me insight into his interiority, why he is who he is.

The anime itself is very character-driven. There's a lot of fighting, but it's never dull because the art and animation are stunning, the dialogue is clever, and the stakes are high. Truly, it is a new favorite TV show of mine, though I am the type of person whose favorites number in the dozens.

Darius cleans up the kitchen. Apart for my quitting debrief, we've spoken very little tonight as compared to usual, but the quiet is comfortable. I light some candles and put some music on, take a few hits of my weed vape, and do a bit of journaling. The music is opera, specifically from *Carmen,* of which we saw a production a few months ago, by the Pittsburgh Opera.

In my journal, I try to capture the feeling of wild, unbound possibility ribboning through my mind. When I'm done with my goal of three pages, I'm quite stoned. My stoner journey does not have a very deep history; it's a development from the last year or so. I doodle a bit in the header space and margins of today's entry in my composition notebook.

Then, from the loopy tangles of my mind, I remember like a flash of genius lightning that I have brownie mix in our pantry cabinet. Though it doesn't even approximate what Darius does professionally day in and day out, I love baking while stoned. It's an activity of creativity and pleasure, small work for large reward, the work being the finding and measuring and mixing of ingredients. Following simple steps, pre-heating, baking. The rich aroma of brownies filling the kitchen, then the rest of the apartment. In my hazy daze, I find myself dreaming up a silly fantasy that the neighbors will walk by our apartment feeling a little jealous as they smell the sweet aroma wafting from my oven, that jealousy inspiring them to make their own yummy treat tonight, to indulge themselves. Then, the effect would ripple until the whole building smells of baked goods, then our whole Squirrel Hill neighborhood, until the whole city of Pittsburgh is baking with me tonight! I giggle to myself, alone in my kitchen.

After mixing my ingredients, I pour the batter from my heart-shaped vintage mixing bowl, into my ceramic brownie pan, sprayed with oily goodness so my box mix creation won't stick. The brownie pan is square, eight by eight inches, and it has an endearingly basic black and cream chevron pattern around the sides, and gold trim along the pan's edge. I use our dark green rubber spatula to scoop and squeegee as much of the batter as I can get into the pan.

I slip the ceramic brownie pan into the preheated oven and take a peek at the clock. I'm feeling carefree, so I don't set a timer. I relish the feeling of this small risk, leaving the timing of the brownie's bake to chance.

The aria coming through our living room speakers is the iconic "Habanera" in which Carmen sings with pride of her own fickleness, her commitment only to her pleasure and her desire, wherever they take her. I appreciate her honest selfishness, how she seems to understand herself, even her most destructive traits.

I have been obsessed with a few of the arias ever since Darius and I saw the show at the Benedum. When I looked up the Habanera aria on YouTube, I was delightfully shocked to see that the Carmen in the production featured in this particular recording was peeling an orange as she sang. In the production I had seen, she had also been peeling an orange. This had been my first time at the opera, and I hadn't known how much of the opera was written, how much of it always performed more or less the same way, besides the music and lyrics. *This choreorangeography blows me away,* I think as I watch each sensual motion of the mezzo-soprano's hand intently.

Carmen's motions peeling the orange are a nuanced story unto themselves. She is sensual, yes, but there is tension, decisiveness alternating with indecisiveness, pensiveness. Listening to this rendition of "Habanera" now, I try to tap into that patient sensuality of Carmen's character. She might not always know what she wants, but she's confident that whatever it is, she *will* have it, no matter the cost.

Time to lick the batter, I tell myself. This ritual has long been one of my favorite parts of baking. Though I was acceptably thorough with the spatula, there are still plenty of batter swirls along the inside of the heart-shaped bowl for me to enjoy, and the spatula itself has plenty of the dark, rich stuff still clinging to it.

Taking Carmen's spirit to heart, I grab my phone from its place on the kitchen counter, the music in the living room seeming to surround me in my stoned state, the familiar strings thrumming in my blood. I open my selfie camera, lean my phone against the dish drying rack, and press record. *The Food Freaxxx are going to love this.* First, I give the green spatula a simple lick, enjoying the bit of thick sweetness left there from the ordeal of getting most of it into the brownie pan. The weed has me feeling in a state of heightened sensation. Licking the spatula, with an aria from *Carmen* playing in the background, alone in my kitchen— it all arouses me. Nobody is here to see me indulge in sweetness and decadence, but if I want them to, they *will.* It's so lux.

I cradle the heart-shaped bowl in my left arm, just resting against my breast. With a flick of my right wrist, I am gathering more dark, thick, not-quite liquid onto the rubber spatula. Now, I lean into my pleasure, into the indulgence I am honoring in my little kitchen, in my little apartment, all just for me.

I close my eyes as I let myself lick along the flat sides of the rubber spatula, then along the edge. Goosebumps raise in a wave of silent susurration on my arms as my tongue catches brownie batter on it.

I scoop the remaining batter greedily onto the spatula and lick it up as if it might just kiss me back. The act of licking, the sweet chocolate flavor, makes me tingle all over. I'm falling deeply, erotically in love with myself right now. I let myself feel the profundity of this pleasure, of refusing to deny myself this moment, horny and licking brownie batter alone in my kitchen. It's like a dance; I find myself swaying from side to side, still cradling the bowl, swiping the rubber spatula and then licking it in a perfect rhythm I'll probably never be able to replicate. I get lost in my reverie, let myself give in to it all: the taste, the sensation of the batter against my skin, my tongue, the performance for the camera. My cami comes off, I cover my nipples in chocolate and drag my tongue across their ecstatic peaks, I smile at the digital reflection of myself in my phone, free.

Once the batter has dwindled so that it is unscoopable, I toss the spatula into the sink gently. I swipe a finger along the surface of the bowl's inside to gather up the final traces, then lick and suck on my fingers deliciously, setting the bowl down into the sink and stopping my recording.

I run my hands under warm water from the kitchen sink, then cup my hands to fill them with enough to cover the lower half of my face. I rinse off the lingering traces of chocolate as best I can, then wipe my face on the fresh tea towel Darius hung from the oven door handle yesterday. I put my cami back on and head into the living room. Already, the warm chocolate fragrance is spreading through the air like magic.

I saunter over to Darius, who is busy in his little computer corner. I wrap an arm around his neck and kiss the top of his head. He removes one side of his bulky gamer headset. "Something smells good." I see him note the heat in my eyes.

"I made brownies and they made me horny," I blurt out. I feel a weird combination of triumph and bashfulness.

Darius laughs. "Wow. Someone's embracing their inner Food Freak" he says, turning towards me in his rolling office chair.

"Oh yeah," I purr, my mouth now inches away from his as I lean into him. "I'm going to post the video right now."

"Video?" Darius' eyebrows shoot up, and he squeezes my ass. "You're becoming incorrigible." He presses his lips to mine slowly and I lean into him. Our tongues meet. Always intoxicating, my Darius.

"You taste like brownies," he says.

"I licked the bowl clean," I explain.

"I want a lick." Darius cocks his head to one side and ravishes me with his eyes. He's not talking about the brownie batter.

"I think we have another 20 minutes or so until the brownies are done."

"Plenty of time to get a good licking in," Darius says. He gives a devastating pause. "Let me finish this game first."

I make a bratty wordless whine in protest, but feel my core pulse at the way he's denying me. He knows what he's doing, knows I love to be teased and made to wait.

I let out a huff and stalk over to the other side of the room, throwing myself onto the couch once there in a soft flop, all brat.

12

Vic's Idle Hands

I'm. So. Bored. I glance up from my phone and glare at the ceramic unicorn planter that sits on the dining table I found on the curb, holding a pothos that has seen better days. The unicorn smiles at me, the plant's vines drooping from the top of its head, begging for a pruning with its many sad, yellow leaves. The thumb is always greener (in my mind) when I'm plant shopping than when I'm actually caring for my plants at home.

Today and tomorrow are my days off. Well, technically right now *is* tomorrow— it's 3am. Working the late shift at the store has further exacerbated my night owl tendencies, and ever since Alan and I split, there just isn't enough going on to keep me from feeling crummy or thinking crummy thoughts.

I sip my Dr. Pepper and refresh my email. Nothing. No calls, but that's expected. No one ever calls anymore. No social media notifications. I toss my phone across the couch. It lands face-down and I glare at my phone case, which has a unicorn on it jumping through a rainbow, plus a sparkly sticker of a pair of purple skates. Social media, sure, it's fun, but not after doom scrolling for five hours. Enough already. But what else is there to do? I sigh and pick up the stupid rectangle again.

Something about the breakup has made me horny to an unhinged degree. Part of it is that I miss Alan, yes, but it's the sense of unmoored possibility, too. My future could lie anywhere. With anyone. It's the one upside to the breakup: this feeling of possibility.

The increased libido can in and of itself be an upside, too... sometimes. But a lot of the time, it's too much to bear, often feeling like the longing part cannot be staved off by toys and porn much longer. And I *really* love fucking myself. I am a sex-positive, liberated woman! But I've been hungry to experience more, to experience other people. Literally: hungry.

Even when I was with Alan, I found there to be a sensuality to food. Really, it was something I became aware of when I first started working at the store five years ago, but I only just started to become truly hungry in this way since the breakup.

First, I joined a few sub-Reddits on the subject of food fetishes and "wet and messy" fetishes. Some stuff is up my alley on these kinds of pages, some less so. I really love seeing women make sexy messes specifically with cakes, sweets, creamy and crumbly things of any kind. I'm not really into the videos where folks are covered head to toe in sludge, but I get the appeal, and it does look pretty fun and liberating to be covered in mud or slop.

Finally, I got sick of the landscape of that corner of Reddit, as most of the commenters were apparently men, and not very feminist ones at that. There wasn't much gender diversity in the content to satisfy my greedy bisexual proclivities, either. My eyes were ready to roll right out of my head in annoyance some nights I spent scrolling, reading the idiotic comments some of these dudes posted. I decided to dig a little deeper into the web to find a food fetish community I could really be a part of. That's how I found Food Freaxxx.

It's a simple little website where people have to pay a small fee to join. We each pay $10 a month for access to the private online community where we can post photos and videos, chat, even attend live, virtual play parties. I've only been to one play party so far, and I just watched. It was a whipped cream party and it was extremely hot. Some folks were on camera alone, some with a partner. Very creamy, very dreamy.

I stand and stretch. I trudge to my bedroom, littered with various unicorn toys and stuffies. It's nice having my own place. Who knows how much longer I'll be able to afford that in Pittsburgh. Even here, the cost of living sure isn't as reasonable as it used to be. The apartment is dead silent except for the hum of my window unit air conditioner and the occasional ambient building noise. The walls are a disappointing yellowish beige, worse than office sludge grey. I'm not allowed to paint them like I was at my previous place. My old landlord was pretty cool... for a landlord, anyway.

The unicorns serve many purposes. Of course, they, along with the rainbows and sparkles that come with them, are a poetic protest against the drab and dreary "landlord special" wasteland. But, they're more than that. I've always loved them. They're powerful while remaining ever-incorruptible. They're magical, like me. I feel they represent my essence. Of course, it's the kind of thing that, once people know you're a fan, you're doomed to receive gifts with that particular motif for the rest of your life. But being doomed to an eternity of unicorns doesn't sound half-bad to me.

There's also the matter of threesomes and unicorns. In the threesome-verse, the app-scape, as it were, bisexual women looking to be the third with couples made up of a man and a woman are known as unicorns. Sometimes, the term has a pejorative glare reflecting off of it, because, when used by some of those couples, it can connote that those couples will view the person they invite into their bed as an object. *She's not a person with feelings, she's a unicorn. A diamond in the rough. She wants us to ride her over the rainbow.* Or whatever.

I feel like I've reclaimed it for myself. Yeah, a woman like me is tough to find, and some people think that I don't even exist. But I *do* and that is fucking powerful. Plus, I'm sexy, and despite the whole virginal thing unicorns have been saddled with in fairy tales, they're sexy, too. Plus, I think my unicorn stuffie collection is innocent enough as far as dirty little secrets go.

As I open FoodFreaxx now, I see a new video was just uploaded only moments ago.

13

Darius— Uninhibited

Gabby has been eyeing me from across the room with her hand down her pajama pants for the past ten minutes, since I sent her away.

In our one-bedroom Squirrel Hill apartment, my gaming PC is set up in one corner of our living room. My desk faces out into the living room, so in lulls in the gameplay I often will glance over and catch Gabby's eye to blow her a kiss or trade silly faces.

Now though, she is staring intently at me, waving her phone at me, her right hand down her pants making slow, circular motions.

I finish my game and stretch slowly beside my desk, catching Gabby's gaze on the bulge in my neon green briefs trying to poke its way through to her from across the room. She got me these briefs, and I know I look damn good in them. I'm wearing a black v-neck that lets a little bit of my chest hair peek out, along with the Cuban link chain Gabby gifted me a few years ago. I close the space between us, stand beside the couch. Gabby looks up from her phone and smiles bashfully at me, then presses the phone against her chest coyly.

"What's going on over here?" I say, as if I've caught her in the act without her wanting me to, as if she hasn't been throwing come-hither glances my way for the past 10 minutes with her hand in her panties.

"Oh nothing," Gabby purrs. "Just chatting with a new friend about my video."

I feel a delicious twinge in my pants, my bulge pressing harder against the fabric of my briefs. I grip it from outside the fabric in an effort to literally get a grip on myself.

"That doesn't sound like nothing," I try my best to give Gabby a serious look, but it's difficult with the mischief dancing in her eyes reflecting back at me.

She turns the phone around to face me so I can see what she's been looking at. On the screen, it's *her*. As she is now, in her pajama pants, but shirtless and licking brownie batter off a spatula the same way she licks pre-cum off my cock. Playing with it. Swiping it on her nipple and licking it off, gripping her breast and squishing it against her cheek to get the right angle to lick herself. The Gabby in the phone smiles wickedly at me, knowingly— and then I look down at the Gabby on the couch and see the same wicked grin spread across her lips.

Beneath the video, there's a comment: **Looks delicious. And I bet the brownie batter tastes good, too.** I look a little closer and realize I recognize the woman in the profile photo— it's @ViciousVulva, the sexy woman with the fiery red hair, the one whose video we commented on the other day.

"What?" Gabby says, eyes wide with feigned innocence.

"Get your ass in the bedroom," I demand.

She squeals with excitement and pops up from the couch. I give her jiggly ass a playful slap as she crosses in front of me and heads to the bedroom.

Before I know it, she's naked on the bed with her legs spread for me, her phone beside her. I accept the invitation and lay down on my stomach, nestling my head between her legs. I give her a few teasing strokes of my tongue and she sighs against me.

"You wanna see more?" She teases, her tone almost as delicious as the taste of her pussy still on my tongue.

She shows me @ViciousVulva's profile and I learn she's a roller derby babe. Tough and a little experienced as a "unicorn," she knows what she wants.

Next, Gabby shows me their messages. They've been sexting a little bit in the past few minutes. My skin blazes when I read that both of them have included me in the fantasy they've begun to spin in their chat. Fuck, I find myself wanting a complete stranger. I insert a finger into Gabby playfully, gently. She's soaking wet and she gives a little moan.

"Mmm. What do you think of our new friend?" Gabby asks me.

"She seems interesting. I think I would like to get to know her more," I demure.

"Oh really? That's good, because I think she wants to get to know us, too." The mischief in Gabby's eyes glints brighter. She reaches out her hand and I give her phone back.

"I'm gonna film you a little bit to send our new friend, okay?"

"Let's give her a show," I murmur into Gabby's pussy before diving back in.

14

Vic's Newbie

The mention of a unicorn in profiles on sites like FoodFreaxxx isn't always a red flag as far as couples go, not on its own. It's often just a shorthand for what people are looking for. It's all in the way it's used. A brand-new couple who recently popped up on Food Freaxxx, @Gabby_and_Darius, included a unicorn emoji along with a sparkle emoji at the very end of their little "About Us" blurb, which, coupled with the rest of their profile, I found cute. That's why I left a flattering (horny) comment on @Gabby_and_Darius' sexy brownie batter video a little while ago, and sent them a request to chat.

It looks like most of their photos on their profile are of them on vacation, some clearly taken in New York, others somewhere sun-drenched and tropical. There's one where they look a little shiny in the sun and the Brooklyn Bridge is behind them. They're turned towards each other, laughing, Gabby's eyelids sparkling with glitter, Darius' smile sharing a similar spark.

I feel a conflicted twinge of emotions. They seem so authentically in love, even in their pictures, like Alan and I were. I quickly push the thought away and focus on how hot they are. I feel blood rush to my cheeks, and to my clit, as Gabby's first message comes through: **Hey, gorgeous! Thanks for the sweet comment.**

I type: **You have such a pretty smile. And I could totally get lost in Darius' chest hair.**

It's a test. If it's really her, and she's serious about sharing her man, she won't mind me complimenting his chest hair. If she's ready, she'll like it, maybe even try to turn up the heat. She'll be into it. If she's not ready, her jealousy will flare and she will swerve in the opposite direction, changing topics or maybe even ghosting me (which has happened to me before). It's a game of sexting chicken.

If it's not her, and it's in fact the dude pretending to be her, he'll reveal himself sooner or later with an unsolicited dick pic or some other such crass move (which has also happened to me before). I know not all guys do that, but the ones who masquerade as their partners usually are stupid enough to send unsolicited dick pics.

Gabby replies almost right away: **OMG I love burying my face and fingers in his chest hair. It's the BEST. And thanks, I have to say Darius is an expert at making me smile.**

I answer: **That's sweet.**

It really is. It smacks saccharine, but I don't hate it. So like a fellow woman to beat around the bush. I know it's probably her because she turned down the heat with her cute commentary, rather than trying to make a mile out of the inch I gave her. I brought up the chest hair, she liked it, but she fell back on the smile comment.

Gabby: **He's also an expert at making me cum. ;)**

Oh. I feel a rush of wet heat emanate suddenly from my core.

Before I can reply, she fires off another message.

Gabby: **Sorry, is that too much? Also, we're big fans of your ice cream sandwich video.**

I smile as I type my reply: **Not enough. ;) I'm glad you enjoyed my little cookies and cream adventure. How does he make you cum? What does he do that makes him such an expert?**

Gabby: **He's veryyy skilled with his tongue, his hands. He has long, strong fingers.**

Me: **Only his fingers are long and strong?**

Gabby: **Not to be hyperbolic, but his cock is glorious.**

Me: **Glorious?!**

Gabby: **Do you want to see him fuck me with it?**

Just reading this invitation sets me aflame. I feel my heart beat hard and fast and take a deep breath in an effort to ground myself. My desire is suddenly dizzying.

Me: **I would love to.** 😍

I yawn, the sunrise seeping over my ugly walls and into the art prints I've hung with double-sided mounting tape in a half-assed attempt to jazz up the place. I feel good. Gabby and Darius made me feel good, and I haven't even met them yet. I've been in these sexting/cybersex situations before. They usually fizzle out pretty quickly, but I find myself hoping this one won't.

We spent over an hour exchanging videos, them of their lovemaking session, from both of their perspectives, pouting into camera, clearly enjoying the show they were putting on for me. I responded in kind, doing my best to get halfway decent action shots of me pleasuring myself, posing for them with my timer on to take some nudes that I honestly think may have been some of my best work.

Tomorrow is derby practice. I'm looking forward to it, but part of me wishes I could drive to meet Gabby and Darius instead of driving to the rink. I sigh and a shiver runs from my crown to my crotch. It's been a couple weeks since I've gotten laid. That's not *that* long, but I have a healthy sexual appetite that simply needs to be sated.

Last night, Dee was texting me to ask where I want to hang after practice. It's a thing we do as a team, and Dee and I usually try to get on the same page so we can guide the team to an easy post-practice hangout spot. If we leave it up for discussion to the group, the rest of the team takes forever debating where to go. Inevitably, a few people lose interest in hanging out at all, the group shrinks, and half of the folks who stay get annoyed at where we end up going. Dee and I usually suggest our favorite diner. It's surprisingly vegan friendly and they have beer, so it pretty much satisfies the usual complaints or points of contention.

I catch myself fixating on thoughts of eating at the diner tomorrow and realize I need to sate my actual hunger, too, my stomach rumbling.

I get out of bed and head to the bathroom, then head to the kitchen to figure out what I can make with the least amount of effort. I grab my vape pen from the window sill above the sink and take a hit while I wait for my coffee to brew.

A few minutes later, I'm delightfully stoned and making quick work of some tortillas and shredded cheese into a makeshift microwaveable quesadilla, a stoner staple that should hold me until lunch.

I always make it a point to arrive a few minutes early to work. I hate rushing, and I got a talking-to from Bill last year for consistently clocking in three to five minutes late. I can't have Bill up my ass, so now I leave the apartment early, take my time driving, parking, walking across the parking lot. I give myself time to chitchat by the lockers in the back room, check the day's schedule when I walk in.

I go through these motions today, like any other day. I walk up to the large front desk, where the managers conduct most of their business (many of them hiding back there until a customer sniffs them out and bays at them for a return or exchange or some other such demand).

Time has really flown by, and I can hardly believe that I've been here for five years now. Those instances like the one with Bill last year are rare between my managers and me. They like me and some of them aren't *totally* evil in my book. It's not my dream job by any means (no job is), but I leave my work at work, I have a flexible enough schedule that I get to do derby, and I work with some cool people. I've actually made amazing, lifelong friends here among my coworkers.

We have health insurance and most of us can pay our rent without too much trouble, so it's considered one of the best retail gigs in the country. I still think it's worth unionizing to make sure we're getting the best deal we can and to have some sort of protection, but unionizing is a touchy subject with some of the more veteran store employees. That's how the corporate powers that be divide us: a carrot dangling from a stick. You chase the carrot, and when you finally get to stop running, you stop giving a fuck about the rest of the poor bunny rabbits you hopped beside your whole life. When I reach my seven-year anniversary with the store, I'll make the maximum hourly wage I can make. Though I'll be standing on the other side, munching on that coveted carrot, I'll always fight for the newbies. We're all on the same bunny farm here, and we should look out for each other. I keep hope alive that the union thing could still happen for us someday.

I step out of the back room after stopping by my locker to grab my trusty box cutter, clipping its holster to the pocket of my purple work pants as I say hi to a few people, then I glide swiftly onto the sales floor, glancing around to get a quick sense of who I'll be working with. It's about to be three o' clock, so whoever is still here is either about to clock out, or they're in it for the long haul with me tonight: the closing shift. I nod and mumble a quick "Hey" at a few more people as I make my way to the front desk to clock in.

I still have a few minutes to spare, so I decide to take my time and read over the schedule for that day. Something I enjoy about my job is that the day is broken up into different tasks, so I get to move from section to section doing different kinds of work throughout my shift, until the store closes. When that happens, we all pretty much work the load.

I sigh, trying to stave off the annoyed feeling pricking at the back of my mind as my eyes skim over today's schedule, where I see a penciled scribble slashed with neon pink highlighter indicating that I'm training a newbie for the entirety of my shift. I hadn't gotten wind through the gossip mill that we'd even hired any new crew members, so I figure this might be their very first day of the standard two-week training everyone goes through. Normally, I don't mind training new folks, but I'm distracted after my virtual romp with Gabby and Darius last night, not to mention exhausted from stretching my night owl hours even further than usual to ensure we were all properly sated. I had hoped to coast through my shift on autopilot, but now I will be dragged to half-speed as I explain the proper way of completing each task as I go about my day and the reasoning behind the way I do it all.

Suddenly, a perky ponytail and *literally* glittering eyes— glitter all over her eyelids— pop up next to me at shoulder level. My brain hadn't quite caught the name of the person I'd be training; I was so preoccupied with the initial wave of irritation I was trying to break through from realizing I'd actually have to try today, of all days. "Aha! Vic, I found you. I'm Gabby, I think you're training me today?"

I glance down at the name tag pinned to the generous bosom of this person, and it confirms what she just said: **GABBY.** Gabby smiles at me, sparkling. She wore glitter as eyeshadow in most of her profile photos, too, and I watched that pretty mouth shape into some fun, filthy business only just last night.

I'm stumped as to what exactly to say to her right now, surrounded by the bustle of crew members clocking in and out, the customers huffing or dilly-dallying by as they grab a few impulse purchases on their way to the registers. My stomach clenches the way it does before showtime as I study the chipper smile pasted on Gabby's face. I feel like I'm about to get beat up by a bunch of hot babes on roller skates. A flicker of panic ignites in my gut. *Does she not recognize me?* I knew who she was immediately, I have images of her and her boyfriend's naked bodies dancing in my mind even now. Suddenly, I realize I never responded to her initial greeting. Before I can spiral any further, Gabby blurts out in a hushed tone, "I'm sorry, I swear I didn't know you work here. I'm not a stalker or anything."

Unable to control myself in time, I guffaw loudly. A few of my coworkers'— *our* coworkers'— heads swivel in our direction. Gabby's eyebrows knit together with worry and embarrassment. "Oh my God, *no*," I say finally, looking directly into her brown eyes, surrounded by pink iridescent sparkles. "I was actually worried you didn't recognize me," I admit in a quiet voice. I'd at least like to give her a few days to get her bearings before becoming fodder for the gossip mill. The only thing our store is better at than customer service is gossiping, and we're freakin' incredible at customer service. "Is it your first-first day?"

Gabby nods. "I drank so much coffee before coming in. I could barely sleep last night from the nerves and... other stuff..." She stutters a bit, blushing. "I—I'm not used to *starting* my workday at three in the afternoon, you know?"

"Aw, you were nervous?" I tease. I notice that we have an ease between us, though the air feels like it's buzzing with electricity. It's a sexy tension.

"Shut up!" Gabby smiles at me, and warmth fills my belly and cheeks as I feel myself beaming back in her direction.

"Come on, they're waiting for us to come save the day in produce," I say, and we traipse away from the front desk for a day of trainer-trainee bonding.

During our lunch break, we decide to sit outside. It's spring, so there's a bit of a nip in the air, but the sun is out and the sky is surprisingly clear. I'm glad we will have some relative privacy to talk. There are a couple of other crew members nearby on a smoke break, but they're engrossed in their own chat, grumbling about which managers pissed them off today, as we all do every day.

"Let me give you my number," Gabby says suddenly. The warm feeling in my stomach returns, radiating out into the rest of my body despite the brisk spring air. I've been trying to gather the courage to offer her my own digits all day, but between my nerves and being at work, I just haven't been able to find the right moment. I'm grateful she found it for us.

"Definitely. I'll give you mine, too." I say, setting my tiny disposable fork down into the plastic bowl of the salad I grabbed from the grab-and-go section. I take my phone out of the deep front pocket of my favorite work pants and hand it to Gabby.

She sets down the burrito she's eating and wipes her hands on a napkin, then hands her own phone over to me, then studies the rectangle in her hand. "Nice unicorn sticker," she says.

"Thanks," I say, feeling my face heat. "They're my favorite. I, uh, relate to them." *Was that a hint? Am I dropping hints? Do I want to drop hints now that we work together?*

"Nice," Gabby replies, and I focus on trying not to let my face redden any deeper.

My efforts in the toned-down blush department are proven futile by her next words, though. "I'd love to introduce you to my boyfriend, Darius. We should all hang out sometime. I'll talk to him about it." I can tell she's trying to be discreet by keeping her tone light since there are others around, though they don't seem to be paying us any mind.

"Sure," I say, trying to sound nonchalant. *Why am I such a nervous wreck?* I've slept with plenty of hot people and had my fair share of group sex in the last few months, but I feel like my heart might just beat out of my chest right now. God, I think I actually *like* Gabby. "We should head back in," I say, giving myself a mental shake. "We don't want Bill up our asses, and trust me, he *will* be if we clock back in from lunch late."

Gabby shoves the last, too-big bite of her burrito into her mouth. She looks irresistibly cute with her mouth full like that, cheeks bulging and lips puckered together as she chews with concerted effort.

We clock back in right on time and spend the rest of the day in easy conversation, the sexual tension dimmed to friendly chatter in the presence of the rest of the store. As for the job itself, I can already tell Gabby is a natural. She's patient and friendly with customers, energetic and thoughtful in her approach to tasks around the store, and a good listener. She's asked me great questions while I've trained her today. When I clocked in for my shift, I was irritated to be training someone. As I clock out at the end of our shift at 11pm, I'm irritated that the managers usually spread the training out between crew members so that newbies get a healthy variety in what they learn and how they learn it. I want to keep her all to myself. I want to spend time with this woman, talk to her, get to know her...

We walk across the parking lot together to the designated employee section. Gabby's car is a white sedan that's pretty beat-up on the outside. "Damn parking garage," Gabby mutters when she notices my gaze lingering on the scar-like scratches on her doors.

I stand next to my own bright blue hatchback, feeling a little awkward, but mostly not wanting to say goodbye. Finally, I blurt, "Nice job today! You're going to do great."

Gabby smiles at me. "Thanks! I think I'm going to like it here." She yawns, and I remember my own exhaustion the first few times I worked closing shift. "I'll text you," Gabby announces with a sincerity that makes my heart lurch into my throat, then we get into our cars and go our separate ways.

15

Gabby's News

Driving home after 11 on a weeknight through the empty streets of Pittsburgh is a rare novelty for me. My body aches, back, legs and arms sore from moving heavy boxes of apples and sacks of potatoes in produce. My heart aches a little, too, yearning and uncertain. *Vic.* Her name echoes within me, the bisexual demons seeming to chant it in adoring unison.

I texted Darius once today, responding to his message asking how my first day was going. I let him know things were going well, but I didn't mention Vic, thinking that it was likely information better shared in person. Not that I had the time to craft the delicate and somewhat diplomatic text I felt the situation would require, anyway.

When I walk through the old, heavy white door to our apartment, Mimi doesn't bother getting up to greet me. She raises her head sleepily from the dog bed next to Darius' desk, which isn't far from the entrance to our place. I could almost swear she has a quizzical look on her face, as if she's wondering why I'm arriving home so late. I slip out of my sneakers and give her a scritch in the little divot in the middle of her hard forehead.

Darius slips off his gaming headset and gives me a wide smile so warm it could almost relieve my aching muscles. "Hey! There's my hardworking neighborhood grocer," he announces. "How was your first day?"

I return his smile, step into the space between his legs, wrap my arms around his neck, and kiss the top of his buzzed head, the little hairs pricking my lips and chin. I breathe in his scent and sigh. "It was good. It was... interesting." I consider my word choice. "Surprising," I add.

"I want to hear all about it," Darius says.

"Well, do you remember how during the interview process they told me that I'd get paired with different crew members throughout my first two weeks for training?" I say, running my hand across his prickly head.

"Oh yeah, who'd they pair you with?" he asks, curious.

"Uh... Vic," I say slowly. "As in... Vicious Vulva," I add, to clarify.

"Vicious Vulva?" Darius repeats, dumbstruck.

"She works there. She's been working there for like, five years, and she trained me today. We spent the whole day together," I explain, and I feel my cheeks heat at this last bit of information, despite the context being completely innocent and professional.

"Well, that's Pittsburgh for you," Darius says with a chuckle, then sighs. "So typical. You have threesome cybersex with someone one day, and the next day they're training you at your new job." Now, I chuckle. Hearing the absurdity of the situation from Darius assuages the tension and worry in my gut a bit.

"It might be the most Pittsburgh thing to ever happen to us," I agree. Among locals, Pittsburgh is known for being a city with a small-town feel. It's very common to see people you know when you're out on an errand, no matter what part of the city you're from or currently in. It's something I love about the city, running into work friends or Darius' improv friends at the farmers' market.

"How was she in real life?" Darius asks. So, I tell him all about our day together, how easily we got along, how much we laughed together and how patient she was while teaching me. I tell him about how we exchanged numbers, and he seems excited by this.

By now, I've showered and we've moved to the couch. "Let's ask her out," Darius says with a shrug. "I feel like the Steel City gods want this threesome to happen. We must appease them."

"Is it possible that we'll get to fulfill both of our fantasies at once?" I waggle my eyebrows at my boyfriend. To have a threesome during which we also play with desserts sounds exceedingly hot.

"Everything you do fulfills my wildest fantasies," Darius says smoothly, and I smile. Leaning against him, I place a soft kiss on his arm.

It's late, but we stay up for another fifteen minutes crafting the perfect text to ask Vic out on a casual date later this week that will hopefully lead to more, if all goes well. She replies almost instantly, and I'm not surprised she's up at this hour now that I know she's a closer.

Vic: I am so down

16

Darius and the Art of the Three-Person Date

It's finally warm out today, and Gabby's ass looks more luscious than ever in the short, lime-green dress she's wearing, the hem dangerously close to the round bottom of her ass, caressing it with every swish of her hips, in time with her steps. I am hyper-aware of her and our surroundings, more than a little on edge. I hold the tall glass door to the Carnegie Museum of Art and Natural History open for her. I am nervous about what today might hold, who we might be at the end of it all, but I'm excited and definitely turned on.

We walk across the large, white marble tiles of the entrance to the lobby and stand by the modern, black front desk to wait for Vic to arrive. Gabby grabs my hand and holds my gaze. "Hey. I love you so much. I'm really excited about today, but if you change your mind about any of this at any point, it's okay. Please tell me if you feel even a little bit uncomfortable or unsure about anything."

I raise my eyebrows at her, taken aback a bit by her sternness. "Sure... But are *you* okay?" I ask her.

She lets out a huffy sigh. "Yeah. Sorry, I don't mean to be intense. It's just, this was my idea, and I don't want you to feel like you have to go along with it for my sake."

"I'm here because I want to be here," I say. "And I'm the one who suggested our little bargain, remember?"

Gabby inclines her head dubiously, her brows flat. "I mean, come on. Really? What do you really think of all this?" Her tone is piqued with sincere curiosity.

"I think it's gonna be *fun*," I purr, melting my gaze over her. I bring her hand to my lips and kiss.

"You do?" Her eyes have a sheen to them, and I know she is feeling a cocktail of emotions that must bear a resemblance to my own.

"Hey. You know it's okay if you change your mind, too, right?" I say softly. Gabby nods. Her words from the other day echo in my mind, the memory seeming as if from a long-ago dream now. *I don't even know if it's* actually *something I want, or more of a fantasy.* "It's okay if it turns out to just be a fantasy," I add. "Although... I have to say, Vic does seem pretty great." I make my eyebrows dance playfully, and she scoffs, but her expression is mild. She seems a bit more relaxed now, and I feel the sharp edge of my nerves dull a bit.

"Oh, she seems pretty great, huh?" she teases. Then, she head-butts the side of my arm softly. "Yeah, she *does* seem pretty great," she repeats, then sighs dreamily. Dirty clips and messages we exchanged with Vic are replaying in a sort of best-of reel in my head now, and I imagine the same scenes are running through Gabby's own mind as I pull her into me for a hug, leaning my chin on her head.

We pull away from each other and, as if on cue, I catch a flash of fiery red hair in my periphery. I turn my head back toward the glass doors at the entrance to the museum, and see her: Vic, not just a pretty smile or lithe nude body on a screen, not a witty online profile, not a uniformed customer service smile, but a beautiful woman, a person going about her daily life with strong strides. However casual, her movements belie her athletic nature. I notice her muscular calves and thighs as the short skirt of her purple dress flutters around her bottom, offering glimpses of creamy skin. Gabby waves her over, and my gaze bounces between the two of them, the similarities of their wardrobe choices endearing. As if reading my thoughts, Gabby mutters, "Great minds."

I have no trouble at all imagining Vic kicking ass as she skates circles around everyone, though I don't have the faintest idea of how roller derby works.

17

Vic and the Art of the Three-Person Date

Walking into the museum, I notice Gabby's dress has a silhouette similar to mine, a flowy skater mini-dress, though mine is purple with a paisley print. I notice a lot of things about both her and Darius, the details flooding my senses all at once. Their touch is easy, they seem to naturally gravitate towards one another. Gabby has her arms wrapped around Darius' waist. She smiles, her chin upturned to look in his eyes. I don't find it obnoxiously showy or feigned for my sake. It just seems like their genuine, natural way of being around each other. They're cute together.

As if they feel my gaze, they both turn to look at me at the same time. Gabby's smile widens and she waves enthusiastically, her fingers slicing rapidly through the air above her head.

A short time later, we're walking at a leisurely pace through the section of the museum with antique natural history dioramas, many of which date back to the museum's inception. The museum itself is not unfamiliar to me. It's one of the Pittsburgh gems that transplant residents like us typically find ourselves exploring within our first year in the City of Bridges, coming back occasionally for dates or something to do when we have family in town. "Yinz mentioned you're originally from Miami. How long have you been in Pittsburgh?" I ask.

Gabby answers, "About four years. We moved here so I could waste my time writing poems in grad school."

"Don't say that!" I protest.

"Yeah, what the hell?" Darius gives Gabby a sharp look.

"Sorry if I'm a little cynical about my prospects of making a living off of my poetry, jeez," Gabby says, hands splayed in mock surrender. Darius softens his gaze and grabs one of Gabby's hands as if to comfort and steady her.

Picking up the thread of their story, Darius adds, "I came along for the ride when Gabby started at Pitt but ended up finding a job I really love."

"At Buttercream, right?" I recall the detail from the anecdotes Gabby has shared with me. I have actually been to that bakery in the Strip on a number of occasions, and I wonder vaguely now if Darius and I have ever crossed paths before as strangers there. So Pittsburgh.

Darius nods. "What about you?" Darius turns toward me and I notice how darkly beautiful his eyes are, how thick his lashes, but most of all, the intensity of his expression. He seems like the type of person who does things all the way or not at all.

A twinge sticks in my stomach as I think back. Alan's face flickers in my memory, then my first year in Pittsburgh floods my mind in amber fragments. The memories are like honey, a slow drip that catches and almost immobilizes me. Before I let myself be entirely caught up, I answer Darius' question. "Uhh... fifteen years?" I nod as if to confirm the answer to my own question.

"I'm from Mississippi originally. Oxford. I also came here for school, but for undergrad."

"Hail to Pitt," Gabby says in a silly, sarcastic voice, sticking her tongue out to one side and forming two fingers into a peace sign.

We share a giggle and I get the sense that the ice is broken. We continue to traipse lazily through the museum, talking and getting to know each other.

Later, we are walking through my favorite part of the museum, the shiniest, most magical part: the Hillman Hall of Minerals and Gems. This exhibit is set up as a sort of maze of smoky, reflective panes of translucent glass. Under spotlights, as the name of the exhibit implies, chunks of minerals and gems gleam and glitter on tiered displays, each neatly labeled with its name and country of origin.

"Okay, I'm so sorry to be this ignorant, and I admit that I probably should have just Googled this before meeting you..." Darius starts.

I interrupt him, an impish impulse overtaking me. "So dramatic, Darius! The *clitoris* is the pretty little bean-shaped—"

Gabby shushes me violently, but her shush sprays into a sputtering giggle. "Vic, shut *up!*" She hisses, smiling despite herself and glancing around at the nonexistent patrons who might have overheard. It's a slow day at the museum. Darius' face has gone a shade of red as vibrant as the garnets on the shelf across the room. I smile back fiendishly, enjoying messing with both of them.

"*Anyway,*" Darius starts up again after a beat of silence, playing up a feigned awkward reaction at my silly joke. "Vic, I was hoping you could explain roller derby to me."

"Oh! I mean, yeah, Google definitely would have done a way better job than I can. To me, it's a very you-have-to-be-there-to-really-get-it type of thing, but I'll tell you the basics." I take a breath and notice that both Gabby and Darius have their full attention directed at me. I find myself relishing their gazes, wanting their eyes to stay on me longer. "Derby is a very physical sport, very in-your-face. The women I skate with are very passionate."

"And you? Are you passionate?" Gabby asks me, serious heat in her eyes.

I look over at Darius and feel heat from his intense gaze as well. I swallow hard. "I like to think so." I shrug, as if that will stop the pink from rising in my cheeks. "I mean... Yes. I am. I've been told I'm too much, so I guess that's the shitty version of being told I'm passionate."

"Fuck that shit. Passionate people make the world go round," Darius says.

Gabby nods enthusiastically. We finish the loop through the gem exhibit in relative quiet and step back out into the bright antechamber just outside. Directly across the Hall of Gems, in a bright room separated from us only by floor-to-ceiling windows, a couple of archaeologists are on display, working. *What a strange world we live in,* I think to myself.

As if reading my mind, Darius says, "Do you think the dinosaurs could have predicted that their ancient remains would end up in a place like this, where tourists pay money to watch archaeologists study their bones?"

Gabby and I laugh, then Gabby protests, "Hey, our tickets are for more than just that, and it's important to support our local museums!"

"Yeah, yeah, I know," Darius grumbles good-naturedly.

"Should we grab something at the café and hang out for a bit?" Gabby suggests.

Once at the café, we all decide to get regular coffees. When the barista hands them over, Gabby grabs a cup and Darius grabs the other two. "How do you take it?" He says, and I think I catch a mischievous glimmer in his eyes.

"Light and sweet," I answer, decidedly enjoying this little act of care.

"Noted," Darius says. While they busy themselves at the cream and sugar, I find us a table outside by the water feature. It's a modern, rectangular pool with a dozen or so jets of water fountaining a lovely melody of white noise. I'm facing a bustling Forbes Avenue, my back to the museum's massive, dark glass wall. Plenty of university students hustle by in groups, apparently taking advantage of the long-awaited warm May day. It's not uncomfortably hot, the row of tables by the fountain pool are under full cover.

I don't have to wait long before Darius and Gabby join me. Darius hands me my coffee and I blow into the little hole in the lid before taking a tentative sip. It's perfect, exactly how I like it

 **18**

Gabby and the Art of the Three-Person Date

There's such an ease between the three of us, and my curiosity is piqued, so I muster up the courage to ask Vic, "What made you say yes to hanging out with us today?"

Vic's smile is made even more beautiful by the soft blush that rushes to her cheeks. "Well, we had some nice chemistry. Plus, it's practically a rite of passage in our line of work to fuck a coworker." She slaps the table and laughs heartily. "I'm half-kidding, but have you ever seen *The L Word?*"

"Not yet, but it's on my list," I say, my eyes drifting to her purple sparkly nails, cut almost to the quick, adorning her fingertips that rest against the sides of her coffee cup.

"Well, in the show there's a web of all the sapphics in Los Angeles. They're all linked by who they've dated and slept with. The store is kind of like that." Still staring at her hands, I imagine what her touch might feel like.

I snort a laugh, hoping I can play off my staring. "You paint quite the picture." My gaze shifts to my own hands now. In a panic earlier, I cut and filed the three middle fingernails on my right hand, effectively botching what remained of my last fancy manicure for who knows how long. I left all five long on my left hand since it's not the dominant one. My "research" tells me I'll *probably* only need two fingers if things go well today, but I couldn't make a confident estimate as to which two I'd prefer on my dominant hand, so I cut down and shaped all three candidates, short and smooth, just to be safe.

Darius pipes up now. "What about me? I'm not a member of your grocery store sex cult."

Without missing a beat, Vic says, "Like I said. Chemistry." The look she gives Darius now sends a rush of heat to my core. She turns her gaze on me and I sense that she's studying me, looking for something on my face, maybe jealousy? But all I feel is desire— for her, for Darius, so I send a knowing smile back at her.

Vic's cheeks redden again and she takes a deep breath as if preparing to tell us something. "I went through a bad breakup about six months ago. I mean, I'm still going through it in a lot of ways. My ex kept my dog, my apartment, which we lived in together for years... It's been a lot."

Her tone is casual as she says this, as if she's used to the pain, the story that cracked her life always needing to be held at arms' length. "I'm so sorry," is the only thing I can think to say, trying to convey my earnestness as my eyes meet Vic's. My gaze flickers over to Darius, and in his own eyes I see fire, a righteous rage on Vic's behalf. I hope for his own sake that Vic's ex never crosses my boyfriend's path. He does not stand for the mistreatment of anyone he cares about, and judging by the look on Darius' face, today just put Vic on that very short list.

Vic shrugs at my sympathetic remark. "Don't be. I'm okay, or I will be. I joined Food Freaxxx and some other apps as a sort of fun distraction at first, but then found myself discovering new things about me, what I'm into. It all started to feel a lot deeper than I thought it would, or even could."

"I think I know exactly what you mean," I say softly. Then, before my courage can vanish as quickly as it just appeared, I add, "Do you want to show us what you're into?"

We arrive to the hotel in separate cars. A few minutes after we park, Vic pulls up next to my beat-up sedan in her little blue hatchback. I put down my window and gesture for her to do the same. When she does, I say across the asphalt distance, "Come over here, Darius has something for you."

"Jeez, can't he wait for us to actually get into the room?" Vic quips.

I snort. "Not that! ...Yet." Darius chuckles, too. Vic turns off her car and lets herself into our backseat.

"Is this the part where you kidnap me?" Vic says.

I whip my head around to face her. "Don't even joke like that!"

She smiles. "Relax. You called me over here to do drugs right?"

I return her grin, and now Darius turns to face her in his seat, revealing the glass pipe he brought with him as if it's a secret treasure. With a few second-nature movements, he has the bowl packed. After a couple puffs from each of us, the car is packed, too— with fragrant smoke.

I cough helplessly into the crook of my elbow as I cross the parking lot, leaving the two professional stoners to get on their own level while I, the amateur, check us in for the night— "us" being just me and Darius, as the record for the booking of the room with just one king bed officially states. No need for nebby hotel employees to know what we're getting up to tonight.

When we texted Vic to ask her out, Darius and I had decided that we'd get a hotel if she decided she did indeed want to have a threesome with us. Something about neutral territory felt safer for our fledgling mission outside the secure walls of monogamy. Plus, I felt it would add a little extra classic spice to the whole scene, the two of us fucking a near perfect stranger in a hotel. Vic feels far from a stranger now, though.

In the hotel room, Vic slides herself backward on the king-sized duvet, pushing herself up against the fluffy pillows. I watch her shuffle her body into a comfortable criss-cross position, then shift her mane of fiery curls to rest on one shoulder, wrapping around the back of her neck and leaving the other side bare. *Bare:* the word echoes in my mind. *The skin where her neck meets her shoulder must be impossibly soft,* one of my bisexual demons whispers. I lick my lips, dreaming of the kiss I hope to soon plant there. I find myself wanting to say something, but am entirely at a loss for words.

I climb onto the bed and kneel, attempting to be... polite? I have no idea what the right way is to go about this. Darius sits at an angle on the side of the bed to my right, just out of reach. He's watching me intently. A queer sense of absurdism at how funny and bizarre life is bubbles up in me and I giggle nervously. I glance at Darius, who snorts good-naturedly, but he couldn't know why I'm giggling, could he? It's possible he does know, that he can read easily on my face the disbelief at the surreal scene in which we now find ourselves.

Vic giggles along as if she's in on the joke, too. "What?" she says. "Just your average Thursday night, right?" I guess my feelings really are that transparent.

A surge of panic threatens to overwhelm me, as I once again doubt that I'll have the faintest clue of what to *do* with this woman. *Shit. I talked a big game online, but pleasuring two people is more than a little intimidating.*

"Right," I agree, giving her a nod and a big grin. Then, realizing I've regained my ability to speak, and before I have the chance to lose my courage, I hasten to ask, "Can I kiss you?"

Her eyes sparkle above her dazzling smile and she nods eagerly. I lean forward and crawl a couple of paces to reach her. On all fours like this, I meet my lips to hers and give her a trio of sweet pecks. *My first time,* I think to myself. *Lips to lips with a woman,* a chorus of my bisexual demons sing-swoons. "You're so soft," I breathe against her mouth. I pull away slightly and look into her eyes. They are still smiling at me. I watch her eyes drift to the spot to my right, behind me, where I know Darius is still sitting on the edge of the bed. I swivel my head along her sightline until my eyes reach his. Darius' eyes move from my gaze over to Vic and back again.

"Hi," he says.

"Hey," Vic and I say in unison. Our jinx moment sets us off giggling again. Darius crawls toward us now. I kiss him, then watch in awe as he and Vic come together like magnets in slow motion. Butterflies knock the walls of my stomach with the rush of this new experience. Darius kisses Vic deep, like he means it, and I reach out to touch him. I feel him hard as a rock in his jeans, and it sends a surge of awareness to my core. I hear both of them inhale and exhale hungrily.

I remember my urge from a moment ago to kiss Vic's neck, and decide now is the perfect moment. As Vic and Darius' tongues meet for the first time, I press my lips to that spot where her neck meets her shoulder.

"So soft," I whisper in her ear. I know I'm repeating myself, but I can't help it. I'm stunned, mesmerized.

She makes a soft noise that is a blend of acknowledgment of my comment and a response to the devastating way Darius is set upon her mouth. I lick her neck in an attempt at a motion I hope embodies as much softness as the skin it touches. Vic sighs with pleasure into her kiss with Darius, then turns toward me. She angles her head to meet my lips, and now her tongue is softly pushing and pulling on mine.

I'm filled with an overwhelming need to feel her all over me, to witness her and Darius all over each other. I find myself too excited at the feast of pleasure that we are about to indulge in.

I let Vic's kisses pull me in toward her, and I move to straddle her. I grab her hands and place them on my breasts, on the outside of my dress. I fumble for Darius' hand from beside me and place his hand on my ass at the spot it's just peeking out from under my skirt, cheek *bare,* because I decided to deviate and wear a thong under my short dress today, instead of my usual high-waisted panties. His hand skates across skin, his fingers tease at my thong string, loosing a little moan from me.

Darius, Vic, and I all take turns kissing each other, and as we do, the gropes and caresses become more free and impassioned. My hunger grows, my wetness driving me to the point of madness, until finally I break away from a kiss with Vic to ask, "Can I taste you?"

"Yes, *please,*" Vic breathes into my mouth, the scent of her breath deliciously intoxicating, like candied smoke. She promptly moves to take off her dress, and Darius helps her get it over her head. I try to drink in every inch of skin, every detail of Vic like this. Her deep purple bra is sheer lace, her nipples pointing at me as if to beckon, as if to dare me.

I decide to take off my dress, too. I start to tug at it, then feel Darius' sure movements take it over my head. He gets up off the bed to undress while Vic and I reposition ourselves. She gets into a more comfortable position, laying down on her back, me on my stomach with my face between her legs. Now Darius lies down beside Vic. He kisses her passionately and caresses her breasts tenderly.

Now, I kiss at the center of Vic's soft panties, a silky deep purple bikini brief with a lace trim. I kiss her thighs, which are as smooth and supple as cream. Hooking my fingers into the waistband on either side, I pull gently at her panties, and she lifts her hips slightly to help me take them off. I toss the panties away, onto the floor.

Vic has her legs open for me while she and Darius get hot and heavy, her round breasts and pink nipples now fully exposed, Darius having shoved the cups down for better access. Between her legs, more pinkness exposed, I notice how she glistens. I slip my arms under her thighs to grab hold of them, lean into her, then taste her for the first time all over again.

I kiss Vic's clit softly, slip my tongue out from between my lips to taste, as promised. The first stroke of my tongue is tentative. I want to please her so badly, I want her to like every bit of contact our bodies have. I want to taste her slick and spread it all over her pussy, to make a mess of us. So, I do. I dip my tongue down and taste her wetness, which has a taste of flowers and acid with a hint of earthy salt, what I imagine a lemon blossom might taste like freshly picked. She tastes divine. I lick, and feel myself finding a rhythm while exploring the shape of her. I want my mouth to memorize it forever.

Vic moans and we meet eyes across her torso. Without stopping the motion of my tongue, I moan into her, offering a response to her call. Darius is watching me intently. Completely naked, he's stroking himself with sweet, dark, intention now. I see an idea light up his eyes, then he moves himself off the bed decisively. A moment later, I feel his familiar, big hands squeezing my ass and tugging at the waistband of my thong. I shift my body to help him pull them down all the way, feel the soft mesh brush all along my legs, then tickle the tips of my toes.

Darius grabs my hips and nudges me into position so that my ass is in the air, my legs slightly spread. My face, of course, is firmly anchored between Vic's legs. She continues moaning, grabs gentle fistfuls of my hair, and grinds her soft, wet pussy against my mouth, fucking my face earnestly.

Darius' hands caress my ass and thighs. He brushes his fingers against my exposed pussy. "I'm gonna lick you now, okay?" He checks in from behind me, then leaves a sweet kiss on my right ass cheek. Mouth still pleasantly full, I make a noise of enthusiastic consent into Vic's pink folds, and the vibrations of my voice in turn make her moans grow more desperate.

Darius' tongue is on me now. I can't see him, but based on how he is holding me, I can tell he is standing to the left of the bed and leaning into me, his arms wrapped around my thighs to support his position. His tongue is teasing. He knows so well what I like, what drives me wet and wild.

19

Darius' Threesome

I've never heard music sweeter than the sound of Gabby's and Vic's moans intermingling in what I can only hear as perfect harmony as I lick Gabby from behind, her own face buried between Vic's legs. As I lick her, I grip her hips and gently rock her between me and Vic, so that she's fucking both of us at a pace set by me. Judging by the pitch of her moans, it's having the deliciously maddening effect on her that I intend. I could stay in this moment forever.

"Baby, please fuck me," Gabby says to me over her shoulder before going back to work on Vic, and I note that she is adjusting her position slightly in order to add a couple of fingers into the mix, using them to thrust into Vic gently.

I pause my licking momentarily to say (brattily), "I *am* fucking you."

"Please," she pants. "I need your cock." As if summoned by name, my cock twitches in response, and I'm glad I'm already undressed because the need to be inside Gabby is suddenly overwhelming.

My need grows to an ache when Vic adds, "Me next," her voice breathy.

As I shift to kneel on the bed behind Gabby, I somehow have the presence of mind to banter and reply, "Please, please, ladies, one at a time."

Vic shoots back, "Oh honey, we're *way* past that."

We smile at each other as we lock eyes over Gabby's arched back, and the playfulness in her gaze grabs hold of something deep inside me as I notch myself at Gabby's entrance.

Even in such an unfamiliar scenario, slipping my hard length into Gabby makes me feel as at-home as I've ever felt. Gabby hums greedily between Vic's legs and a groan rumbles from deep within me as I slide back and forth slowly, not retreating all the way, letting Gabby get used to the fullness of me in the way she's taught me she likes best. I feel her body relax ever so slightly and recognize it as the usual cue that she's ready for more. I rock into Gabby at a steady pace, shifting my weight into her enough that my motions carry over into the way her mouth is fucking Vic, once again setting the pace, fucking Gabby into her.

Vic watches me intently over Gabby's back, her forehead shiny with sweat and her eyebrows knitted together thanks to the sweet torture Gabby's tongue is doling out. Vic bites her bottom lip as if trying to prevent herself from coming undone. She licks the spot her teeth just grazed before asking me "Does her pussy feel good, Darius?"

The friction of my cock inside Gabby gets impossibly hotter in response to Vic's words. A rough "Oh yeah," is all I can manage as reply.

She fists Gabby's hair gently and directs her gaze to my lover licking dutifully between her legs. "You're such a good girl taking that hard cock while you lick me, aren't you?"

Gabby's back arches and she pushes her ass up against me insistently in response, moaning wild, wordless affirmations into Vic's pink softness. I drive into her in earnest now, the slap of skin on skin adding a percussive undertow to the music of their moans.

After a brief and perfect eternity, Vic says, "I would like a turn as the middle of this yummy sandwich, please." Echoing the comment we made on her Food Freaxxx video, Vic's words send us into another giggling fit.

Gabby and I break away from each other, palms and knees sinking into the hotel bed-cloud as we shift. As in the beginning of our session, the three of us press together with kisses and caresses, my tongue grazing and lips sucking at both sets of their nipples as they tangle their own tongues together in a passionate daze.

"I have an idea," Gabby drawls, her gaze darting between the two of us as she alternates showering our faces with kisses. "Do you want me to sit on your face while Darius fucks you?"

"Ooh, that sounds nice," Vic says, and I give my cock a couple of fisted pumps in time with my acquiescent nod.

"Lay on your back," Gabby commands Vic softly. Vic does as she is told and I feel goosebumps cover my skin as I watch Gabby mount Vic's face gingerly while facing me, lowering herself so that her knees are on either side of Vic's face. The position is so familiar to me, it's one Gabby and I have practiced countless times in our own lovemaking sessions, but seeing her sit on someone else's face sets my skin ablaze, and the expectant look she gives me only makes me burn hotter. I feel myself actually blush under her gaze as I spread lube over my cock. We discussed ahead of time and decided we're all comfortable going raw today, the women on birth control and all of us recently tested. The feeling of suspense between us is almost palpable.

Do you want me to sit on your face while Darius fucks you? Her words echo in my mind as my eyes try to process that's exactly what's about to happen— is already happening. Gabby's words reverberating in my mind are punctuated by a little moan that escapes her now, in response to Vic's hungry mouth moving beneath her. Vic looses a grumbly sigh and grabs at Gabby's thighs, seemingly settling in for the ride. I don't miss Vic's knees dropping to either side of her, legs spreading as wide as they will go, an unmistakeable invitation for me. Gabby doesn't miss it either. Her gaze drops to the space between Vic's legs and she leans forward, touches Vic ever so gently, drawing her slickness up and circling her clit slowly once, twice, meeting my gaze again on this final motion.

Before I lose my courage, I notch myself at Vic's entrance and push in ever so slowly. *"Fuck,"* I groan as her pussy welcomes me for the first time, the word perhaps as drawn-out as it has ever been on my lips.

Until now, Gabby is the only woman I'd ever been with. Being inside of Vic feels familiar, but also *different.* She hugs my cock deliciously, and I take my time with these initial strokes, giving us both time to get used to the sensation. A moan that sounds like a plea escapes from between Gabby's legs as Vic's hips roll upward to take me deeper, urging me on. Gabby has a wicked look on her face as she intently watches the place where Vic's and my body meet, but the look melts into something desperate and primal as her own hips roll to intensify what she's getting from Vic. Gabby's head lolls back as she surrenders to the sensation, her hands mindlessly playing with Vic's breasts, cupping them and pulling at her nipples greedily.

After a long moment, Gabby's head rolls back up and she leans forward, reaching for Vic's clit again, now fucking her face in earnest. She matches the rubbing rhythm of her fingers to the pace of her ride and I try to match my own strokes into Vic as their moans climb to a higher pitch and crescendo in volume. I hold onto Vic's soft hips for dear life as I pump into her, Gabby's gaze melding with mine with white-hot intensity.

I feel Vic come apart around me just as Gabby's face breaks into my very favorite expression of hers: sheer ecstasy in pleasure. I suddenly doubt reality, surely I must be in a dream if both of these gorgeous, incredible women are coming at the same time, sharing a bed with me. *How can this be my life?* I can practically feel the powerful force of their orgasms crash over me like a wave, the impact reverberating throughout the room, throughout the universe.

Once the orgasmic frenzy subsides, Gabby swings a knee over Vic's head carefully to dismount. Vic licks her lips as if savoring every drop of my girlfriend's pussy and wipes at her brow with the back of her hand. Gabby pulls at my shoulder at just the right angle to nudge me onto my back beside Vic, and I obey wordlessly, trying to catch my breath.

"Did you come good?" I ask Gab. She nods, a huge grin spreading across her face as she settles into a position so deliciously familiar to me, head between my spread legs, ass in the air, her elbows propping her up as she grips my cock with one hand. She gives it a sweet kiss on the head and I use one hand to reposition the pillows beneath my head to settle into a more comfortable position.

Vic scoots in closer to me and nestles under my other arm, playing with my chest hair as she sprinkles kisses on my cheek and neck, her tongue occasionally darting out to tease my earlobe. As she does, Gabby licks the pre-cum off my tip, then licks her lips generously before using that tip to trace the wet shape of her mouth. After a few circles, she opens her mouth and tastes me, licking me and then closing her lips around my head teasingly.

Gabby gives an appreciative hum that I swear I can feel vibrating through the core of my being. "You taste like Vic's pussy," she says approvingly before sliding more and more of my length into her wet, warm mouth.

Just then, Vic kisses me deeply. As we pull away, I say, "Vic tastes like *your* pussy." Vic gives me a sweet smile and a little peck on the lips before sitting up. "Where are you going?" I ask her. In answer, she simply moves to all fours, her round little ass in my face as she covers my chest with gentle pecks that could almost be interpreted as innocent, if she weren't marking a path down my belly, to my inner thighs... to meet Gabby.

Gabby's grip on my cock gives way to Vic's, the two of them kiss, their tongues converging, wet and fervent, at my tip. They take turns taking my length deep and I groan with each grazing motion at the back of their throats. Vic's sweet pink pussy is tempting me, taking up the view of my entire right side. I reach for her with a tentative middle finger, swiping at her wetness with a feather-light touch as Gabby's head bobs up and down on my length in earnest. Vic's hand is pumping in perfect rhythm with Gabby's blowjob, and Vic turns to look at me over her shoulder and nods, her eyebrows once again knit in what I already recognize as her signature, tortured plea.

I sink my middle finger into her gently, then let my index finger follow, matching the pace they've set. We press on like this in tangled ecstasy and I lose control swiftly when I feel Vic come apart on my fingers again, her sweet, slick cunt clenching around my fingers. The realization that I've— *we've*— made her come twice today, coupled with the intent, dutiful pace they've set upon me, sends me over the edge.

"You two are going to destroy me," I say as they straighten to kneeling positions to kiss after Gabby swallows me down.

20

Vic's Threesome

I have lost count of how many orgasms I've had at this point. We're all resting, actually cuddling sweetly on the bed together, Darius the littlest spoon with me in the middle as Darius' big spoon and Gabby's little spoon.

Cuddling soon turns to caressing which soon turns to kissing with lots of tongue. Before it can get too heavy, I sit up, pulling away from both of them, and blurt out, "I brought a surprise with me."

Both of their eyes go wide, and Gabby smiles, playful curiosity dancing in her eyes. "Does this have anything to do with whatever you put in the mini-fridge when we got here?"

"Huh?" Darius says drowsily.

"Nothing gets past you two," I tease, shaking my head at sweet, oblivious Darius so he knows I'm pointing the sarcastic tone of my observation at him.

I grunt my way off of the bed, my already-sore body sinking into it with each motion. When I triumphantly dismount the white-sheeted behemoth, I become aware of how sweaty I am as I stand on solid ground for the first time in hours. "First things first," I announce. I walk over to the corner of the room where my stuff is and bend down to rummage through the tote bag I use as my purse for a scrunchie. "Glad I didn't need this," I say, pulling out the hot pink mace key chain I always carry.

"Jesus," says Darius.

"Being a woman is so exhausting," Gabby sings in a purposely silly, off-kilter tune.

I shrug. "I always have it." I release it back into the tote bag void, my hand finds my scrunchie. I put my mass of auburn curls in a quick messy bun, and turn toward the mini fridge to my left. I bend down to grab my surprise.

"Now you're really showing off. What is this, *Legally Blonde?* 'Bend and snap?'" Gabby quips.

Still bent over, I play along. "Beeeend," I say, drawing the word out like Elle Woods does in the movie. In a series of quick, swift motions, I grab the surprise, shut the mini fridge door, and pop back up into a full standing position. "... and snap!" I hold the can of whipped cream up like it's a fabulous prize on a family friendly game show, except I'm obviously in my birthday suit.

"Ohmygod, yes!" Gabby immediately squeals. I walk back over to the bed.

"What's this all about?" Darius raises a bushy eyebrow at me. His eyes and brows really get to me. There's something so profound and romantic there, in the expressiveness of them.

"Don't you love sweets... chef?" I tease Darius.

"*Please* don't make me think about work right now," he says, his eyes dancing with dark mischief. I laugh. I'm beginning to understand what Gabby meant when she shared with me that though Darius is a man of few words, getting to know him is more than worthwhile. His eyebrows are raised now, a slight smile stretching the edges of his mustache.

"I picked this up on the way over here," I say by way of explanation. I give the can of whipped cream a shake, uncap it, and squirt a little swirly mountain of its familiar sweetness into my mouth. I toss the cap across the room with a limp wrist and wanton abandon. It bounces off the wall and lands on the lifeless-grey hotel room desk.

I swallow and wipe at the corners of my mouth ungracefully with my middle finger, then give it a little suck to get rid of the excess cream.

The room has only been quiet for a moment, but it feels like it's been much longer. I didn't anticipate feeling so vulnerable in this moment. I wanted it to feel a lot more casual, and not like a formal *proposal.*

I try for a save. "Anyway, no pressure. If we're done for the night, or if we wanna go another round *without* the whipped cream, that's cool. But I brought it with me in case we really hit it off." I shrug with forced nonchalance.

"Are you really this nervous to ask us about this after coming all over both of us? After meeting us on a food fetish site?" Darius finally says. Gabby and I burst out laughing.

"I'm in," Gabby says perkily.

"Yeah, I could go for a snack," Darius agrees, then reaches his hand out toward me, a wordless request for the can in my hand. I pass it to him.

Gabby is half-sitting, half-reclining on a pile of fluffy white pillows against the headboard. She's mostly covered by the duvet, but her gorgeous breasts are exposed, resting on the blanket.

"Lay flat," Darius commands Gabby gently. Her breasts shift slightly when she does, both of them bouncing into a rounder version of themselves in this position, her nipples forming into delicious points. The whole bed shakes a little in time with his shaking of the whipped cream can, in turn jiggling Gabby's tits. My mouth starts to water a bit and I feel my own nipples harden against the cold hotel room air in anticipation.

Gabby squeals and giggles as Darius pulls the duvet down and squirts a dollop on each of her nipples, then trails a rather long squiggly smile along the width of her belly, just below her breasts.

He turns his dark eyes on me now. "Are you just gonna watch or are you gonna help me with this?" His tone is playful. Why do I trust this man I just met so damn much? Why do I feel like we could be great, lifelong friends?

I crawl across the giant bed over to Gabby's right side, since Darius has claimed the left. We face each other on our knees with Gabby between us, and we lean over Gabby to kiss each other without saying a word, just naturally gravitating toward each other. He tastes rich, animal, his mouth layered with all the hedonistic secrets we just shared with each other.

When we part, I look down and see Gabby watching us patiently, a genuine smile on her face. She's looked blissed out pretty much this entire time. "Enjoying the view down there?" I ask her.

"Oh, absolutely," Gabby replies without hesitation, nodding her head, which makes her creamy tits jiggle. That sight sends a rush of slickness to my core and spurs me into action. I bolster myself with my left arm in the pile of pillows and use my right hand to gently hold her breast around its sides.

On the drive to the hotel from the convenience store I stopped at, I had envisioned a long, drawn-out tease, but we've been fucking for hours at this point, so in the moment, I decide to give in to my voracious appetite for my fantasy scenario, and just *go for it.*

Instead of licking the whipped cream, I press my lips into it. In fact, I press my whole face into her breast and let the whipped cream make a mess on my face, spreading to my chin and nose. I feel so indulgent, so free. I let loose a long, low moan that becomes a chuckle.

Now I set my tongue and lips to work to "clean" the mess I made, sucking and licking and swiping my whole mouth all over her breast, continuing to inhale the sticky-sweet, melting substance. "Mmm. Is that yummy?" Gabby asks, between soft moans, one hand between her legs.

I talk out of the side of my mouth, the rest of it full of her nipple. "Oh yeah."

I manage a glance at Darius and see for his part, he is nodding furiously in answer to Gabby's question, his mouth also full, his head making her breast jiggle gloriously. I can see his mustache is covered in whipped cream.

Somewhere beyond my titty-addled ecstasy, I remember the squiggly smile Darius drew on Gabby. It seems Darius has a great mind that thinks alike, because just as I set my tongue to work licking the smile off of her, I meet his dark eyes across her belly. We swipe our tongues further down along the squiggly sweet path, meeting in the middle for a sloppy kiss, our mouths unapologetically full as we sit up a bit to kneel over Gabby. I feel a bit of whipped cream drip down my chin and neck.

As we kiss, I send my hand down to Gabby's pussy, slip one finger in, then another, pumping into her. Darius joins me, rubbing her clit. Gabby moans deliciously, her tits and belly shiny with stickiness.

I feel messy and I love it.

21

Gabby's After

It's not a far drive back to our place, but I'm having plenty of difficulty keeping my eyes open, and I can see Darius blinking against similar exhaustion as he tries to keep his eyes on the road.

I wish we could have spent the night with Vic in that hotel room. My weariness dulls the longing I feel, but it's definitely there. But, we hadn't planned on staying the night. We had reasoned that we weren't sure it would be the right move for us, that we didn't know how we'd feel after the threesome, if it did in fact end up happening. Plus, our fur babies needed us back home. Mimi needed us to take her for her last walk of the day, and both her and Groovy needed us to be there in the morning to feed them breakfast. Had I known I would feel this disappointed to part ways with Vic, I would have arranged for a neighbor to help us out in exchange for a few bucks or some Buttercream goodness courtesy of Darius, perhaps.

My heart pangs thinking about Vic going home to her empty apartment, no Ollie to greet her thanks to her asshole ex. Darius yawns next to me.

"You want me to drive?" I ask.

He shakes his head no. "We're almost there. I'm gonna crash so hard when we get home."

"Me, too," I say, nodding in agreement, then add, "As long as it's not a moment sooner," gesturing to the road with just my chin when he looks over at me. We share a weak chuckle. "We expended a lot of energy." He yawns again, and it's contagious.

It's a relief to get home. I leash Mimi, take her down the elevator and outside to do her business, then bring her back up into the apartment. I'm grateful to find Darius already done showering when I walk back into our place with Mimi in tow. He's toweling off his buzzed head as I unleash Mimi and say, "Can you wait for me?" He knows what I mean without further explanation. He dresses and sits at his computer, cueing something up to occupy himself while he waits for me to shower before we head to bed together. *Poor thing,* I think, my own eyes glazing over as I notice his zombified stare into the computer screen.

In the shower, it's as if the hot water and the steam themselves activate a meditative state for me. I watch the water stream against and between my breasts and remember Vic's and Darius' mouths all over them at the same time, their eyes locked on me as they licked and sucked on my nipples. Through my sweet exhaustion, my body pulses with pleasant aftershocks and I sigh in delicious surreality. I douse myself with every detail of our threesome adventure.

It feels a little silly to have doubted my sexuality. I feel validated and sure of myself, but I knew myself before laying a finger on Vic. No one can define my sexuality but me, and no one can ever take it away from me. I wish I had the energy to journal right now, but I settle for trying to commit the experience and this feeling to memory while it's all fresh, echoing in every part of my body and being.

Darius follows me to bed a few moments after hearing the water stop running, no doubt, and we cuddle close and tight, face to face, breathing each other in. I resist the urge to debrief right there and then. I know when Darius' heart desires quiet, and I give in to what the moment requires of me. We have forever to talk about the experience, to decide if it's something we'd like to repeat, to hash out details of shoulda-coulda-wouldas. It can all wait until morning.

Right now, we are basking in the afterglow of damn good sex and pleasurable new experiences. I hear Darius' breathing slow and deepen as he lets himself drift into slumber. I nudge him to turn to face the other way and he does, aware of my cues even in sleep. I hold him close, playing the big spoon. Tonight, the comforting weight of sleep finds me more easily than it has in weeks. I sigh and wake up to golden light and soft, bearded kisses.

 **22**

Darius' Mind

I kiss Gabby a few times to wake her before I head off to work. I woke up with a lot on my mind, overwhelmed with emotion. That happens to me sometimes. I feel a lot, mountains of feelings like tangled threads, not really sure how to make heads or tails of any of it. Big feelings take a while for me to process; it's always been that way for me.

Gabby has described to me that she feels like she has a constant emotion-scanner in her body, able to check in on how she feels and name the feeling, finding its root. I guess they forgot to install the emotion-scanner when they made me in the people factory, I don't know.

My tangled mess of emotions always undoes itself on its own. I imagine my subconscious does all the work. I wake up not understanding myself, and then some time later, sometimes as long as a few days later, the emotions are unraveled, then neatly spun and spooled into thoughts, ready to be woven into different tapestries: understanding, action, conversation— Conversations with myself, and oftentimes with Gabby, too.

Gabby wakes in response to my kisses. She smiles and kisses my lips instinctively. "Morning," she grumbles.

"Hey, I gotta go. Are you gonna wake up or keep sleeping?" I ask.

She groans. "Keep sleeping. I don't work until three."

"Okay if I make something easy for dinner?" I ask.

"Of course. There's freezer stuff... in the freezer," she says groggily. I can tell she is fighting sleep just to string these simple words together.

"Sounds good. I'll make that," I play along.

Sitting in a corner seat on the empty, early bus to work, scenes from last night play in my head, spliced together like an avant-garde porno film shot from my perspective. *Well, I can check that off my bucket list,* I joke to myself, the urge to experience it all again sending a twang of pleasure through my body. I notice I am still considerably tired from the night's activities as I lean a shoulder and the side of my head against the big bus window.

One thing Gabby and I have in common is that we don't really believe in regrets. Did I have an amazing time last night? Hell yes. Do I hope that she and Vic did, too? Of course. One of my tangled emotions suddenly reveals itself to be worry. I'm *worried* that Gabby didn't have a good a time as she seems to have had. Or, possibly worse: As I'd feared before, maybe Gabby did enjoy herself in the moment, but there are unforeseen, delayed emotional repercussions that have yet to reveal themselves to her, to us. I suppose I shouldn't discount the same possibility for myself, or even for Vic, whom I find tangled up in my worry along with the rest of my inner tangle.

I get off the bus and begin the short walk from my stop to the bakery, trying to switch my brain into "work mode." Many of my early morning tasks are quite rote, so work mode right now just means all the brain-space I'm not using is still available for me to think of Gabby, how she's feeling, and how good it felt to be inside her and Vic. Their mouths, their spit, their wetness. I look around nervously at the almost-empty bakery. Only Rebecca is there with me, working. I know she can't read my mind, but my thoughts are so dirty, they make me paranoid.

I can't think straight; clearly, that's not my strong suit. I find myself suddenly emotional, thinking about the queerness of our threesome. Even though I didn't have sex with another man last night, there is no denying the queerness of last night's events, overall. It's like I experienced homoeroticism by proxy, and I feel connected with my queerness in a way I hadn't in a long time. *Fellas, is it gay to have a threesome with two women?* I joke to myself, thinking in meme format. The answer comes to me swiftly, as if divine: *It is if you want it to be.*

When I'm at the final stage of decorating a cake, I enter a meditative state. My eyes follow the soft, swift motions of my hand, squeezing the piping bag with expert pressure to release the curly, full streams of icing on the cake as I turn it round and round on the platform with my other hand. My motions are delicate despite the heavy metal burly brute I appear to be (and, in many ways, am).

I'm grateful to have an adventurous, generous partner who wants to share these types of experiences with me. Gabby. My heart and my groin swell as a flashback to our night with Vic shoots through my mind. Gabby experienced ecstasy in a way that I had never witnessed before. This isn't to say that I think she doesn't experience pleasure when it's just the two of us. I couldn't count the impossible multitude of orgasms we've given each other if my life depended on it. The novelty of the threesome, though, watching her give in to her desire with such abandon while doing something for the first time— I'll never forget the look on her face when she came that night, her pleasure-tortured eyes piercing my soul as Vic clenched around me.

Seeing her blissed out like that was an honor, but it knocked loose in me a certain curiosity, a feeling like something is missing for me and I'm not sure what. What I *do* know is that something is up inside me. I feel a churning in my gut. It's *want*. This threesome made me realize I want something, and I don't know what. As great as the want, though, there is also guilt. In Gabby, I have everything I could ever want in a partner. To want anything more feels wrong, ungrateful.

I give the cake a final, slow spin, appraising my work, noticing the tight feeling of my brows knitting together. I box the cake up, my head hazy and stressed. Sorting through my thoughts is a burden I hate most days, and today is especially annoying. I shove the guilt away since it feels antithetical to the experience of the threesome. Wasn't this whole bargain brought about by not being afraid to want more?

I go through the familiar motions of setting the boxed cake in the back room's fridge, taping the order Rebecca scribbled and the receipt I printed to it, ready for the customer to pick up later. Soon after, I'm on my way back home, blasting Zappa in my headphones on the bus.

Once home, I take a nap to ensure I'll have enough energy for improv class, but not before I touch myself, reliving moments from last night as if I can taste it. Exhaustion washes over me after my release.

A shiver covers my body as I walk from the bus stop to Improv N'at. I'm not shivering because it's cold. The first hints of summer warm the buildings on either side of the street, golden light peeking through the clouds during the late sunset I'm currently enjoying on my walk. The shiver is my body's visceral reaction to the flashbacks I'm experiencing right now, flashbacks of the absolutely beautiful filth I got up to yesterday with Gabby and Vic.

It feels strange to be walking about in the world after experiencing such bliss, such hot hedonism. I feel like a god— or at least the luckiest mortal to have ever lived— to have experienced such goddesses, such beautiful women, in their most vulnerable states, in such abandoned pleasure. The sheer level of trust they continue to place in me turns me on. I feel my cock swell a bit and take a deep breath to steady myself. I'm looking forward to improv class more than usual today because I feel the need to get out of my head.

Though it's lovely to envision Gabby's and Vic's naked bodies every time I close my eyes, my lack of presence in the current moment has me feeling off balance. Improv is good at bringing me back from that surreality, at grounding me.

As we walk up to the bar above the theater after class, I notice I am feeling a lot more at home in my body and mind, clear-headed. My friend Aaron and I walk beside each other. He's telling me about a video game he tried recently.

"I think you'll like it. The music is really good, and I know you love that shit. It's on sale, just get it and come play with me, bro."

Come play with me, bro, echoes in my mind. Aaron and I have no sexual tension between us whatsoever, but that phrase, on a man's lips, threatens to fog my mind with filthy thoughts all over again. I force my attention back to my conversation with Aaron.

I put my hands up in mock surrender. "Alright, alright. I'll buy this stupid game. But if it sucks, I *will* complain and give you shit."

"Yeah, yeah." Aaron dismisses me with a wave of his hand. "Typical Darius. You're gonna like it, but you need to come into it with an open mind. I feel like you're already determined to hate it."

I stop walking and wiggle my fingers near my forehead, then make a bursting motion with my hands, commanding, "Mind: open!"

Aaron rolls his eyes and half-groans, half-laughs, and we keep moving.

It's nice hanging out with improv friends at the bar. When I first started taking classes, though I had fun, I still held my classmates at a distance. Being with Gabby always made me feel like I had one person who understood me, but spending time with Vic has made me feel like maybe the world is a bigger, kinder, less lonely place than I thought. It doesn't have to be me and Gabby against the world. The world can be more welcoming, or at least neutral, than that. Being jaded is overrated.

I have a light beer and a zillion glasses of water. I don't really drink, but I'm a thirsty guy. Aaron and I socialize with the rest of the group, letting our friend Libby hold court. Libby is unhinged and hilarious. I love doing scenes with her because she's so uninhibited on stage. Plus, she's a really experienced improviser. She's taken all the classes at Improv N'at, plus a couple of others at the other theaters in town. She's in our class now just as a bit of a refresher, and to have fun.

When I arrive back home, Gabby is lounging on the couch, hair wet, fresh from her post-work shower, scrolling on her phone while one of her comfort sitcoms plays like white noise on the TV. She looks up at me, sending a sweet smile my way as I shut the front door behind me.

Mimi gives a jealous, complaining groan, her tail slapping the couch a few times as she eyes me kissing Gabby hello. I give her a pat on the head by way of greeting.

"How was class?" Gabby nuzzles against me as I sit on the couch.

"Fun. I need to shower. I'm only gonna sit for a sec," I tell her.

Gabby makes a wordless whiny noise in protest.

I kiss the top of her head and smooth her hair with my hand. "How was work?"

"Work was fine. Honestly, it was a blur. I spent most of the day in the produce section staring at apples and prepackaged salads, wondering if what happened last night was a dream."

"Replace arugula and Granny Smiths with delicate cake piping and cannolis and you pretty much have my day in a nutshell, too," I confess.

23

Vic's Tale of the Dog

My phone vibrates. It's Alan. "When are you going to pick up the dog?" Not even a *Hey* this time. I sigh, knowing I must really be pissing off the man I love. Loved? He barely even sounds like himself; I can't recall ever hearing him use this tone with me before, even in the thick of our breakup. I guess we're still breaking up, thanks to me. Indignant heat rises up inside me.

I ignore his question, his acid tone. "I'm doing okay, you know, training hard for Hairy Pitts. Work is—"

He cuts me off. "Vic," he practically spits, my name a curse on his lips. He lets loose a rush of air so loud I have to pull the phone away from my ear a bit. "I have really tried to be patient. I love Ollie a lot, but at the end of the day, he's your dog and your responsibility."

My voice sounds small and choked up as I say, "I thought you loved being a dog dad." It was something he often beamed about when we were together.

"I did, but Ollie is yours. Don't you miss him?"

My chest goes cold and hollow at the accusation. *I abandoned him...* "Of course I miss him. I just thought I would... come home to him." I feel pathetic admitting this to Alan. It's too vulnerable, especially after all these months without really talking to him.

"Vic. It's been six months. I'm moving out of this place and I need to tie up loose ends."

The cold hollow feeling in my chest grows deeper, wider, like the pot holes all over this city that expand every winter. Patching them over seems futile; they always resurface. *I'm just a loose end he needs tied up. Cut, more like.*

"You're right," I try my best to make my voice sound like ice and steel. "I'll come get her when I get a chance. I'll let you know." I hang up before he has a chance to respond. I don't want to commit to this. I don't want him to ask me when I'll come.

I'm not ready. I'm not ready to accept that he doesn't want me back home, that soon, it won't even *be* our home. It will just be another apartment. Maybe another couple will move in and get *their* happily ever after. Or maybe they'll have their hearts broken, too.

I'm with Dee at Ritter's, our diner. We don't have derby practice today, just hanging out and shooting the shit for the most part. Really, I called her to hang out because I need a boost of support right now. "Alan called me," I blurt out just as she shoves a few fries into her mouth.

Without missing a beat, Dee, full mouth and all says, "What does that bastard want now?"

I can't tell Dee the full truth. Nobody but me and Alan know that I *purposely* didn't take Ollie with me. I told everyone he insisted on keeping him, despite him rightfully being my dog. I never thought things would go this deep, last this long.

I mime with one finger that she now has a mushy piece of potato on her lip, then continue as she wipes off the gross bit of dismembered fry. "Closure?" I feel my voice lilting up into a question without meaning to ask it. "He wants to talk," I try again, willing myself to believe it's not a lie by way of a vague bullshit technicality.

As if reading my mind, Dee says, "You really think you're ready for that?"

I cast my gaze down at my sweating glass of icy Dr. Pepper. "I don't know." I shrug. "It's been over 6 months. I don't feel fully ready to talk to him, but I've been feeling better than I have in a while and I want to ride that momentum."

"Ha!" Dee guffaws darkly. "Feeling better huh? I bet momentum's not the only thing you've been riding," she teases.

I roll my eyes. Something deep in me wants to *share,* but the impulse isn't directed at the plate of dinner pancakes in front of me. I want to tell Dee about my experience with Gabby and Darius. She knows all about my escapades in the past months, but this feels different, like a precious secret. Everything about Gabby and Darius feels different.

"Wanna hear about something *fun* I did?" I let the word *fun* drip with innuendo as it rolls off my tongue.

Dee immediately takes the bait. Her eyes bug out and her eyebrows stretch upwards in a cartoonish expression of scandalized intrigue. "Oh, *do* tell," she shrieks, not caring that the people at the next booth over are shooting us a look now. We try not to be obnoxious, but we're naturally loud— we can't really help it.

Suddenly I feel self-conscious, an unusual sensation for me, who prides herself on being shameless. *I'm the fucking Vicious Vulva,* I think to myself before taking a breath and launching into my smutty story.

When I'm done, Dee is beaming a smug smile in my direction.

"What?" I protest, unable to keep the giggle out of my voice.

"I knew it."

Now I scoff. "Oh, you knew it, huh? That's impossible."

"Well, I didn't know exact details, but I knew *something* was up. I knew you had fucked." As these last words drop from her lips, she crosses her arms almost defensively, as if anticipating my denial and wanting to spar with me about it.

Instead, I giggle. "That obvious, huh? I guess I've got that orgasmic glow about me!" I toss my red curls over my shoulder in mock coyness.

The playful giggle in my throat catches and falls dead mid-flight as if it were a moth coming into contact with one of those zappers. Alan just walked into the diner.

Dee follows my stunned gaze and turns her head. "Oh," she says flatly, turning back to me.

Alan doesn't see us at first, giving me a moment to study him. As one expects with exes, he is the same yet unmistakably different. My Dr. Pepper threatens to burble back up as I think to myself, *He looks so relaxed, so at ease.* I hate him for it.

His hair looks a little shaggier, his scruff is grown out in a way that seems intentionally effortless. The hostess is power-walking in our direction now, leading him to a table, and his eyes finally lock with mine. I flinch, expecting him to flay me verbally right there in front of everyone in the diner. To use the same acid tone from over the phone the other day, but worse, because he's standing right there, I don't even have distance to filter the sting.

He doesn't. "Hey," he says without a hint of anger in his voice, and it feels too loud to me, as if all the conversation in the diner and the Hoobastank playing on the radio have been dampened, as if every sound but his voice is coming from another universe altogether.

The hostess, seeing that he's held up, points out his table and he nods, cueing her to walk swiftly away.

"Hey stranger," I reply, immediately regretting it. *Fuck, I sound like I'm flirting.* Really, I was trying to come off as casual, even a little caustic because we *are* strangers to each other now, and it hurts.

"You look good," Dee says.

"I think that's my line," Alan replies, too smoothly. I don't remember ever thinking he was smooth before.

"How are you?" I manage to croak. I take a sip of my Dr. Pepper to quench my dry throat and hang on to my cold glass in case my hands decide to start trembling.

He ignores my question. "Sorry I never wanted to come here with you. I started coming here a few weeks ago on my own and I get the appeal now. It reminds me of you, which is nice. And the food is actually decent. Plus, it's a nice bike over."

"I know the food's decent," I practically growl. He really did always pitch a fit when I suggested coming here for dinner. He's kind of an online review foodie snob. I used to think it was a cute quirk of his, but ever since we broke up, I've been enjoying frequenting the spots he never wanted to visit with me.

He smiles and sighs, shrugging in mock surrender, fingers splayed in the air. A long pause weighs in the air between us. "I'm sorry about the other day," he says sheepishly, his voice dropping to an almost-whisper. "I was just frustrated."

Why is he apologizing to me? Words fail me, so I just nod in a show of accepting his apology. I feel some of the tension in my shoulders relieve as I sense our interaction coming to an end. He's not going to ask me about Ollie in front of Dee, and I am so grateful to him for it.

Dee's voice cuts through my soliloquy of gratitude and relief. "How's Ollie?" The question is like a shard of ice flung into my chest.

Something darkens in his eyes, but he just says, "Good. He misses his mom a whole lot." Something about it doesn't feel like an accusation this time. He's being the bigger person, reaching out an olive branch. He always was the gentler one, the more level-headed of the two of us. He turns his gaze back on me and continues calmly, "Whenever you get a chance, you know, you can come get him."

Dee's eyes widen in my direction. "Yeah, I know. Thanks," I say quickly. Why do I feel rage burbling up inside me? I feel so exposed, naked without my lie to protect me.

As if sensing that fury, Alan sighs defeatedly and goes to sit at his table without another word.

I turn back to Dee and try to change the subject as fast as I can. "Did you remember to bring cash?"

Dee dismisses my question with a wave of her hand. "Vic, what the *fuck?* You said he was practically holding Ollie hostage, that he wouldn't let him go. Didn't he kick you out of your apartment?"

For the first time since the breakup, I can't think of a single thing to say.

Our apartment was our sanctuary. I was all too happy, a year after we started going for walks together— a year of dates, laughs, movies, derby bouts— to invite Alan to come live with Ollie and me. My space was slightly nicer than his, and I was more set in my ways, having lived in the converted mansion apartment for about three years, whereas Alan was newer to the neighborhood and to his apartment. Plus, there was nice storage for his bike in the basement.

I thought Ollie would remind him of me.

I thought he would wonder what I was up to on his daily walk around our neighborhood.

I thought he would see my shoes by the door every day, the curtains and rugs I picked out, and miss me.

I left it all behind hoping he would ask me to come back.

My grandmother used to say, "Don't cut your nose to spite your face." I think I left the whole tip of my nose on my pillow, in the bed we shared.

All these weeks, months, as I've been scrolling on my phone, checking out women, men, and couples online on various apps and platforms, even sexting Gabby and Darius, Alan's name has popped up on my phone as he's tried to reach me, images of him and our not-too-distant past life together popped up in my mind. Interrupting my happiness. Interrupting my life.

I've been negotiating with myself. At first, I told myself that if he didn't beg me to come back after a month, I would accept the fate of our relationship. I could manage by taking my aggression out at derby, I told myself.

A month came and went. He texted me to see how I was doing, I replied hoping that the conversation would take a romantic turn, but it never did. After a while, I stopped answering his gentle *How are you?* texts. Then, the texts turned into flat-out demands for me to come get my stuff, then angry, all-caps messages in rapid succession for me to come get my shit.

I blocked him. From my phone, from my mind, I couldn't bear

to see his name or think of this bitter end he was forcing on me, on us. I tried not to think about Ollie too much, told myself he was as much Alan's dog as mine, he could take care of him for awhile, he didn't mind. I tried to ignore the pangs of guilt and longing for my sweet pooch, my little white shadow who followed me everywhere.

I unblocked him. I rented the cheapest, most depressing apartment with a month-to-month lease I could find, telling myself that there was no reason to spend tons of money on a new place since I'd be going home soon, once Alan came to his senses.

I lied to everyone, including myself. It wasn't hard. It felt good, or at least, better than the truth made me feel. I'd stayed in that apartment because it's what I felt I deserved. If Alan didn't want to love me, I didn't want to love anyone else, including myself, so I began to self-destruct.

It's funny, people say to follow your heart, but my lust is what started to lead me out of the void. When I matched with Gabby and Darius, I was expecting a distraction, and I got that, yes, but we really connected. Even though we've only spent one full day together, I feel like I can be myself with them. I can ask for what I want and be heard. I want them and they want me back.

I never knew sex could be healing and validating in this way, until I met them. They have their relationship, but I don't feel like I'm outside of it.

It's like their relationship is a home, and I am a houseguest, being offered the best hospitality and warmth a host can give. They give me shelter from myself, they give me pleasure, we drink each other in and experience sheer decadence together.

Suddenly, I feel sick. My stomach churns with guilty bile. *I lied to Gabby and Darius.* Hell, I lied to half the crew at the store.

Seeing Alan in the diner has certainly rocked me. I envision him and Ollie now, happy without me. *What am I doing?*

With a few more expletives sprinkled in, this is the very question Dee asks of me now. I tell her the truth, and though she is angry with me, I know she will forgive me. She loves me and she knows how tough the breakup was on me. She offers to come with me to pick up Ollie and all the shit I left at the place I used to share with Alan, but I tell her I still need time.

She shakes her head now, our lengthy conversation finally coming to an end as she pulls up in front of my building to drop me off. "You're going to need to sort this out, or it *will* bite you in the ass, Vic," Dee says as I get out of the car.

I turn to face her. All I can say is, "I know." Then, I close the door and she drives away into the night.

24

Darius is Totally Casual

Gabby starts bringing Vic home with her from work sometimes when they have two closing shifts together back to back. Vic stays over, we share our favorite shows and movies with each other, we cook meals together and go out to eat sometimes when no one feels like cooking.

At first, as I once did, Vic found the way Gabby constantly pauses whatever we're streaming so we can share our personal commentary exceedingly annoying. Now, she finds it endearing, or at least that's what I tell myself. In any case, she can't help herself from chiming in with her own thoughts most times.

Vic and Mimi absolutely adore each other. It makes my heart ache seeing her interact with our pittie, knowing how much she must long for her own little Ollie. When I think about her situation and try to put myself in her shoes, I consistently conclude that I would destroy anyone who stood between me and my dog. Now, anytime she drops a little detail about her past life with Alan, I'm filled with rage, even if it's something innocuous and not about how he screwed her during their breakup. I hope for the sake of my pristine arrest record that I never come across that dude, because, for the first time in my life, I don't trust myself to keep that confrontation strictly verbal.

Soon, Vic starts staying over on the nights before her days off. We go for walks in the neighborhood or in the park, we have even gone dancing together once. Vic's days off don't always coincide with Gabby's days off, while my own schedule varies at the bakery and has only gotten more chaotic as we've entered peak wedding season. So, occasionally Gabby and I spend time one-on-one with her. We checked in about it and decided it was fine. It was a surprisingly chill conversation in which we essentially concluded that since we've both watched each other have sex with Vic countless times at this point, knowing the other is doing it alone doesn't feel very strange at all. The whole thing feels normal, totally casual.

Months go by like this, the three of us spending time together in different configurations. Vic's presence even seeps into my time alone with Gabby most days. She's around so often that when she's not, we find ourselves talking about her or reminding each other to tell Vic about experiences we think she'll appreciate as anecdotes later.

It turns out Vic is a great cook and she can smoke me under the table, her tolerance for weed unmatched, a true stoner. On one of the nights when Gabby was working and Vic was off, we got especially zooted. She introduced me to her favorite Bongzilla album and it blew me away. Our sex was slow and passionate that night, every thrust laden with meaning I couldn't put actual words to if I tried. By the time Gabby got home, we were zonked in bed, dead to the world from our tiny deaths. All I remember after our orgasms is waking up with Vic spooning me from behind and Gabby's head nestled in the hollow of my neck. The scene was bathed in golden sunlight, the spell unable to be broken even as Groovy started to loudly demand food from the bedroom doorway, of course sensing that I'd awakened.

For the most part, I've stopped worrying about what it all means. Instead, I worry that if I think about it too much, the spell will indeed break. And maybe I've been smoking too much with Vic, but I'd rather live under this spell forever, even if that forever can exist only in the eternity offered by each present moment as I take it.

25

Gabby's Mess

I can hardly stop myself from grabbing Vic's ass as I stand next to her while we clock out. Darius has devised some kind of surprise for us today, and it's all I've been able to think about ever since he texted Vic and me about it a few days ago in our group chat, which has been buzzing lately. We were working late together and Darius was at home taunting us with naughty messages. That same night, he said he was planning a surprise. Whatever it is, I hope it involves me all over both of them. I want to taste them. I want to be decadent with Vic and Darius and forget everything else.

I drive us to Darius' and my place, where, incidentally, Vic left her car earlier this afternoon when we carpooled to work together. It just made sense since she spent the night last night.

I unlock the old wood door with the bad paint job that leads into our apartment and burst into the space, Vic almost getting caught in the backswing of the door after it bounces off the wall. I apologize quickly and then herald to the living room in my best sing-song voice, "We're ready for our surpriiise!"

Darius enters the living room from around the corner, where the kitchen is tucked away. "Well, hello to you, too," he says.

I kick off my shoes and Vic follows suit, familiar with how we do things in our home by now. I traipse over to Darius, who meets me in the middle of the Persian carpet that serves as the centerpiece of our living room, a gorgeous gift passed down to us by his parents, by far the most luxurious and expensive thing we own. His grip on my arms is firm as we kiss hello, and I hold my tongue as I watch as he and Vic exchange the same gesture, sending a wave of heat over me that soaks into my very skin.

"Is our surprise in the kitchen?" I blurt, but as I move to pass him and enter the other room, Darius stills me with the hands he has wrapped around my arms.

He's wearing a poker-face smile that doesn't budge as he speaks. "You're not going anywhere. Go shower first. Both of you." His tone is commanding in a way that tears me in half— one half wanting to rebel against whatever he says brattily, the other wanting to obey his every word so he'll reward me for being a good girl. "After you shower, you'll get your surprise." He pauses thoughtfully. "Okay, what I have planned may also be just a *teeny* bit for me, too," he admits. He holds up his thumb and index finger in an almost-pinch as an expression of the teeny bit of the surprise that's for him.

I look to Vic and she shrugs. "Well, my curiosity is certainly piqued," she says. I nod at her to lead the way, and she slinks off to the bathroom, giving his cock a playful tug through his sweatpants as she turns away from him.

I follow her and feel Darius watching us go. "Oh, and don't bother getting dressed," he says to our backs, and I squeeze Vic's hand then, both of us giggling as we walk into the bathroom and begin to undress. Though we've taken quite a few frisky showers together, we've also had our fair share of comfortable, quotidian showers, intimate in their own way without being quite so explicit. The time we spend together in the shower now falls into the latter category, a sweet shared space, though we probably set a personal record for *least* amount of time spent showering together this go-round. I can tell she's just as eager to get to the bottom of whatever Darius has planned for us.

When we come back out of the bathroom, I see something on our vintage 50's dinette table, which sits caddy-corner to the living room and the kitchen. In the middle of the table, there is a large, two-tier purple cake with rainbow sprinkles and luxurious, frilly piping. The top tier is shaped like a heart, and its sides are draped with extra lavish details.

Vic gasps and rushes closer to the cake ahead of us. I smile at Darius, who has a huge grin spread across his face.

"It's beautiful," I say softly.

"Unicorns!" Vic squeals.

I join her directly in front of the cake and see what she's so excited about. There are three unicorn figurines topping the cake and about a dozen uber miniature such figurines along the sides, like little pinky nail-sized mountain goats hanging off the side of a cliff.

"Thank you," Vic says to Darius, an overcome earnestness in her eyes. She gives him a big hug and they stay holding each other as she turns to face me. He caresses her breasts as he leans down to speak directly in her ear. His dark gaze rakes over me, though, and I feel my head go utterly soft, all thoughts fluttering away.

"I want you to eat it." Darius says quietly, but firmly. Before Vic or I can respond to this seemingly obvious statement, he adds, "from between Gabby's legs. After she sits on it."

We are all quiet for a moment.

"What, no creampies?" Vic jokes.

"That's later," Darius replies without missing a beat.

"How am I supposed to sit on this thing, babe? Are you going to move it?" I ask.

In answer, Darius grabs me by the waist and lifts me onto our table so that I'm sitting on the edge of it with my legs dangling over the side. The table feels sturdy beneath me. Darius then gestures for Vic to sit in one of the empty chairs to my left, so she does, and he scoots the chair back swiftly, footed in soft felt. This places Vic a tantalizing, teasingly short distance away from me. Darius stands behind Vic, massaging her shoulders and caressing her hair, kissing her neck and head, burying his face in her thick curls as she reaches her arms up to hang around his neck.

Taking that as my cue, I swing my legs up and turn myself around carefully, moving onto all fours to face the cake on the table's laminate surface. It's cool and hard under my knees and palms. Darius and Vic slow their movements, watching me intently. Vic is pressing her thighs together.

"Best view in the house," Vic purrs at me.

"Don't you love a front row seat?" Darius asks her.

I focus my attention on the cake. The table isn't huge, so I am able to lean forward just a bit from my current position and lick some icing right off the top layer.

"Is that yummy?" Vic says.

"Scrumptious," I reply, and I mean it. It's light and creamy, tangy, too. "Is that lemon?" I ask Darius, looking up from the purple frilly icing. I see now that he is kneeling between Vic's legs.

"Mmhmm," Darius says in answer to my question, his mouth full. She leans her head back momentarily, tempted to give herself over to his mouth, then snaps it back up to watch me. I can see the hungry anticipation in her eyes. What will I do next?

I kneel on the table, sitting up. I reach towards the cake with my right hand and swipe some of the purple icing onto my index finger, instantly ruining the perfect heart. I make eye contact with Vic, who is moaning softly with pleasure at what I know to be Darius' masterful tongue strokes, wet and always teasingly gentle at first, so soft. Vic is watching me. Her eyes follow my finger as I drag the soft purple icing across and around my nipple. Now I'm using my whole hand to rub the sugary, lemony goop all over my breast.

I repeat the process with my other hand and breast, feeling myself filled with greedy desire to be covered in soft, sweet mess.

26

Vic's Mess

I'm so fucking wet. I cross my legs behind Darius' neck and grind my pussy on his face as he serenades me with warm, indulgent strokes of his tongue.

"Fuck, fuck, *fuck,*" I pant, watching Gabby slowly lower herself into a naked squat over our glorious purple unicorn cake. A minute ago, she removed the three unicorn toppers and giggled.

Now, she sighs with unbridled pleasure as she lowers herself onto the frilly, sugary tower. It isn't graceful at all, which I find even sexier than if she had been. She's so raw, so enraptured and uninhibited right now. I bask in the sheer hedonism of it all.

Gabby repositions herself so that she is kneeling on what is quickly becoming a purple, crumbly, creamy *mess.* She grabs fistfuls of cake and smashes the soft masses into her generous thighs, then swipes her open palms up her curves, over her hips and belly and glorious tits, which already have icing on them. Bits of cake matter go everywhere. I think I see a teeny-tiny unicorn fall to its doom after making brief contact with her body as part of the sweet, cakey sludge-and-crumble.

I watch Gabby's focus shift from herself to me and Darius across her, back to herself and her sweet mess again. She moves again; instead of kneeling, she sits with her ass in the cake, palms on the table behind her, legs spread open and pussy facing me directly. Her eyes meet mine hungrily, then scan downwards, to Darius' head bobbing between my legs, his tongue searching ravenously for my wet pleasure. Watching us, she slides one icing-covered hand between her legs now and rubs her clit.

We both moan and pant, watching each other and languishing in difficult pleasure, difficult because it isn't enough yet. We both see it in each other's eyes, feel it. We need more. Not just messy. Destruction.

I gently clasp the sides of Darius' face with my hands. He understands my signal intuitively and stops, looks up at me, then stands and turns to face Gabby. I stand from the chair, a bit unsteady, and close the space between it and Gabby to stand between her open legs and take her mouth in a deep kiss.

In her purple revelry she had eaten some cake, so she tastes like lemon buttercream, milky and sugary-tart.

I scoop a bit of icing off the pile of cake on the table with my finger and swipe it onto her nipple, as I had seen her do. I lock eyes with her. "Such a mess," I murmur chastisingly, and she gasps with pleasure as I lick the icing off, then suck her nipple, hard.

I nibble and continue sucking on both of her nipples in turn, to the tune of her desperate moans. I feel Darius' fingers feeling their way inside me, the upward swipe of his hand as he finds my entrance, the sensation of two of them sinking gently into me.

Now that he's inside me, I feel the beast within me fully awake, as ravenous as if she had been slumbering for millennia. I pull away from Gabby's nipples with a playful pinch and bend myself towards her pussy. My open mouth makes contact between her legs and I taste pure cake. It's a delectable mess. I lick crumbs and icing from her clit and labia and in response, she grabs two gentle fistfuls of my hair, no doubt covering my curls in icing and crumbs, but I don't care, because she moans louder than I've ever heard her before.

Darius' cock slips inside me as I'm bent over and I moan into Gabby's pussy, which is now covered in my spit and her own wetness, rather than cake, since I did such a nice job cleaning her up. The motion of Darius' cock rocks me into the space between Gabby's legs, and I let his rhythm guide the strokes of my tongue. Our moans are heavy with hedonism and loud with abandon. Our breath seems to synchronize. I look up at Gabby and she turns her gaze from Darius down to me, her face incredulous with the sheer amount of pleasure I know she must be feeling. Her jaw hangs open from the weight of her pants and moans.

"Fuck, baby, just like that. It feels... so... yummy," she tells me. Then I feel her legs shake as her grip tightens on my hair, the string of high-pitched curses streaming from her lips practically gibberish. I keep licking her ferociously until I feel the tension in her body release. She sighs and I straighten enough to give her a sweet kiss without releasing Darius.

"You taste like me," she says.

"You like that?" I ask.

"Yeah. You like how Darius fucks you?" She asks, gently filthy, resting a palm on my cheek and locking eyes with me.

"Mmhmm," I respond, desperate for the both of them, the look in Gabby's eyes setting me on fire. *How can this level of pleasure be possible?*

Gabby pinches my nipples and kisses me passionately while Darius rails me with long strokes that hit with the perfect amount of force, in just the right spot. Darius reaches between my legs and lightly strokes my clit with one finger.

I moan with desperate gratitude for such a good fucking, and Gabby pulls away from kissing me for more of what I like to think of as her *infamous* dirty talk.

"I know his cock feels so good when it's slamming against your pussy." She looks up at him now. "You like her wet pussy babe?"

"Mmhmm," he growls.

"It's so soft and wet for you. Did it taste good?" Gabby wheedles playfully.

"Oh, fuck yeah." Darius says with a big sigh, turning up the speed of his humping ever so slightly.

"Where do you want him to come?" Gabby asks, relentless in her quest for filth, her desire to heighten my pleasure extreme.

I feel myself melting, my thoughts turning to magma, my body radiating pleasure and sweat. But, after a moment, I manage to ask, "Can he come inside me?"

Gabby gives me an angelic smile and nods, then looks up to

Darius to confirm. "You want to come inside Vic's sweet pussy?"

Between pants, Darius manages a "Yes," but Gabby wants more. She's insatiable, even after having come once already. She wants to drive us mad with our desire for each other.

"Yes what?" She presses.

"I want to come inside Vic's sweet pussy," Darius whines desperately.

They continue back and forth with variations of this and it's like a beautifully debauched hypnosis. Every time either of them say *come* or *pussy*, I feel the tense line of my pleasure wind harder, closer.

My moans are full shouts of pleasure now, my orgasm comes in a big wave, washes over my brain. I rest my head on one of Gabby's supple thighs and relish Darius' thrusts. Each time his cock pushes into me, it echoes the pleasure of my orgasm. I moan earnestly and join Gabby in her filthy cheerleading.

"You ready to come?" I tease Darius. "You were so good, waiting your turn. So patient."

Gabby doesn't let up. "I know you want to come in that sweet pussy. I'm gonna lick it up like I licked all that icing up, okay baby?"

That sends a shiver through me, and another heatwave through my core.

"Oh, *fuck!*" I pant.

"Ohhh *yes!* You gonna come again for me baby?" Gabby asks, enthralled that she's struck a chord in me. "You *love* hearing that, don't you? And guess what? I'm gonna give you another orgasm after this one. I'm gonna lick some of his delicious come off of you and finger fuck you with the rest of it as lube."

This filthy promise sends me over the edge. I shriek with pleasure and feel my body tremble hard as, simultaneously Darius' come pumps into my pussy, warm and wet. I feel his cock pulsing. He slips out of me and steps back as Gabby slides off the table and gently guides me onto the pile of buttercream and crumbling cake.

Darius helps me onto the table and kisses me deep and slow while we wait for Gabby to wash her hands in the kitchen sink.

Then, Gabby returns and makes good on her promise. I am pure lava as she kneels between my legs and looks up at me while she licks Darius' release from my entrance. She does it slowly, she is deliberate and makes eye contact with me. She wants me to see and feel everything, easing into her motions so I don't become too over-sensitized.

Now, as if in one swift motion, she stands, pulls me into a passionate kiss, and slides two fingers inside me. Darius comes up behind Gabby and showers her neck with kisses and my arms and legs with caresses. In this embrace, with Gabby's fingers perfectly curved, come-hithering and thrusting inside me, I come a third time. This orgasm is soft and gentle like the tide coming in, like a satisfying denouement. I tremble and whimper and feel the world fall away one more time.

Gabby slips her fingers out of me and I transcend into bliss as she feeds me come off her fingers, licking it off along with me. I taste Darius and myself and sigh deliciously, then kiss Gabby sweetly. She sighs contentedly, too, then turns to give Darius a peck on the lips.

The three of us wash each other in a quiet daze, communicating almost solely by touch and giggle. We soap each other up without much regard for taking turns, amused sounds bubbling up when we find buttercream or cake crumbs in a new, unexpected spot on each other.

Despite the decadent debauchery we just engaged in, or maybe because of it, this moment feels so wholesome. Something blooms in my chest as I think that I'd like to do this all the time— be with Gabby and Darius, naked and giggling and comfortable.

Maybe it's the post-orgasm haze, maybe it's the courage that comes with conquering new territory in our sexual explorations, but as I rinse the suds off my body, both of their hands on me helping the process along, I blurt, "Do you two want to come to Hairy Pitts next month? To... cheer me on?" The words are out before I can second-guess myself. We qualified to face off in the big bout against the Spinsters just last weekend.

The smile that spreads on Gabby's face is made of sheer excitement. I'm still learning how to read Darius, but I think I see amusement and curiosity dance in his eyes now. Whatever is there, it's not unkind, though maybe a little wary. He and Gabby exchange a look now, and I desperately wish I could know exactly what it means, that I could be in on it, whatever it is that lives in that wordless, tender exchange.

Gabby says, "Can we talk about it between the two of us and let you know?"

I stutter a bit as I say, "Sure, of course." I feel heat surge to my cheeks, and it's not because of the steam or the hot water. Right. At the end of the day, this is all between the two of them. I'm just the sexy guest star to their main characters.

"It sounds fun," Darius adds, and my heart sinks a little more. *Is that pity in his voice?*

I manage to say cooly, "No pressure," and leave it at that.

None of us signed up for more than sex, and, though we have ventured well beyond just that in these past weeks, I know my invitation has crossed a line. Going away together for a weekend is a whole different level of intimacy. But, after the incredible time we just had— not just the sex, but the *thoughtfulness* of Darius' surprise gesture— I thought it would be worth shooting my shot.

As the three of us towel off, I force myself to take a calming breath. Even if they don't come to Hairy Pitts with me, I'm still glad we're sexy friends. Even if they never invite me back to their place and I never see them naked again, I'm glad we've had these adventures together.

Still, I can't help my mind from wandering, from wanting more, more more...

27

Gabby's Demons

My lower back aches in a way that lets me know I didn't lift with my knees enough tonight while breaking down pallets. Vic warned me, suggested I use the fabric and velcro back brace they gave me at orientation to help correct my lifting posture. They always give them out to newbies (when they remember to, anyway), but I've never seen another crew member use one except Vic. "I'm serious about not fucking up my body so that I can fuck up other bodies on the track," she'd said to me as we crossed the parking lot at the end of our shift.

Home now, while Darius is in the shower, I play with myself, idly at first, daydreaming about Vic as I let my eyes glaze over the TV screensaver scrolling by. I love teasing myself. My own patience and tolerance turn me on, it's like I'm on my own plane of space-time. I'm suspended in pleasure, yet comfortable and secure. Like a princess on a cloud.

Sex with myself is most definitely sex. The sex educators I follow on social media, and @Poly_Polly in particular, taught me that. Social media scares the shit out of me, but occasionally, I learn a thing or two on those stupid platforms.

Sex with myself is most definitely sex, and I am a gentle and strong lover. I dominate myself, submitting to my own pleasure.

My orgasm floods me with a feeling of classic, pure release. I feel at once empty of thought and fully in my body, satisfied in the utmost pleasure. As I come, I imagine I'm coming all over Vic's soft fingers, pressing into me hungrily.

I come down as if still resting on my soft cloud, my aches dulling a bit for now.

Out of the shower and dressed, Darius sighs as he lets his weight fall onto the couch beside me. "Hairy Pitts," he says unceremoniously, without any kind of ramp-up. I feel like both of us have been avoiding the topic because, not only was our creamy, crumbly adventure the other day a lot to process and come down from, but we both know going away for a weekend with Vic will officially put us in territory that is more than we initially bargained for.

"Hairy Pitts," I reply with a sigh. I give Darius an uncertain smile.

"I'm sure you already have thoughts about what you think we should do," he prompts.

"I do," I croon. "I think we should go for it. What's the worst that could happen? We have mind-blowing sex and get to know Vic a little better and meet her friends?"

"But what does all of that *mean*, though?" Darius' eyebrows arch high on his forehead.

I shrug. "Why does it need to mean anything? We're having fun, we're all getting along, why not just follow our instincts?"

"Because we have no experience with stuff like this, and because initially, all we wanted was a casual, one-night thing, *maybe* a friend with benefits. I never expected to go on a trip with this person." Something like panic laces Darius' voice now.

"'This person?'" I let a little judgment edge my tone. "Honey, I think it's time that we come to grips with the fact that Vic isn't just some person. I feel a real connection with her, and I'm not the one who baked an elaborate cake for her."

"It was for you, too!" Darius protests, then sighs, scrubbing a hand over his face. "Okay, yeah. But I don't know if I want to be a throuple, or whatever. I don't know that I can give myself completely to another person the way I have with you."

"Nobody's asking you to do that. But, again, I think we should just follow our instincts and see where they take us. Everything has gone well so far and we have no reason to believe they won't continue to."

"Famous last words," Darius grumbles, but the corners of his lips are turned upward in a wary smile. "What the hell, I've always wondered what all this derby business is all about."

"Remember, we can always change our minds, we can always leave if we're uncomfortable, and the same goes for Vic. The minute any one of us doesn't want this anymore, we stop, take a step back, reevaluate... whatever is needed in that moment."

Darius nods, then lets out a wicked chuckle. "Why do I feel like we just made some kind of deal with the devil?"

28

Vic's Bruises

It's nice to get some aggression out of my system and I like feeling like a badass. Hell, it's nice to love my body and get some exercise even though my body's more beat up than not these days. But, really, the thing I love most about derby is the community. It really does give me hope and make me feel welcome and loved.

When Alan and I broke up, the derby team were there for me. Yeah, there were some flash-in-the-pan hookups that helped get my mind off things, but everyone on my team, and even some people from other teams in the league who I've known for years, checked in on me. They listened. They validated me and my feelings. They held me as I cried. And because of this, I will always be grateful for derby, will always be a derby girl.

Getting that aggression out certainly helped, too. I shouldn't underplay that. Heartbreak is sad but it's also fucking enraging— maddening, even. And when I couldn't wrap my mind around Alan breaking things off, skating helped me so much. Having somewhere to go and skate round and round and shove people out of my way— to be slammed to the ground mercilessly myself— felt so good. The rage of heartbreak, in my case, came from rejection. There was also the evil voice in my head espousing the sunk cost fallacy. So many of my "best years" wasted just for it to end. I know that's bullshit because I do believe love is always worth it in the end (barring abuse and the like). The rage came from confusion, too. Weren't we happy? Weren't we resilient? Weren't we committed? I don't know when the rough patch became something different, when our relationship metamorphosed into something ugly and unrecognizable. Even now, knowing it's for the best, the rage simmers within me.

I think the final piece for me is the permanence of it all. It feels impossible to get used to forever without the person you thought you'd spend forever with. The lack of "closure," as people love to label it, is hard, too. How could there ever be closure on this open-ended relationship death sentence?

So, getting a little bruised up and doing a little bruising helps, with a dash of "fuck the pain away," to put it in Peaches' words.

Mingling with the aggression today, though, is good ol' faithful anxiety. I invited Gabby and Darius to Hairy Pitts and I still haven't gotten an answer from them as to whether they'd like to come or not. I've seen Gabby at work but we haven't had much of a chance to chat one-on-one and I am loath to be the one to bring it up. I invited them, and I know they'll get back to me with an answer on their own time.

They might reject me. I try to let the thought glance off of me, tell myself it doesn't hurt. Maybe I shouldn't have put myself back out there so soon, even for mind-blowing, literally delicious, sex. Nothing ventured, nothing gained.

I decide to check my phone while on a water break and, as if on the same frequency as my thoughts, when the screen comes to life in my hand, I find a text notification from Gabby in our group chat with Darius. I take a quick look around to ensure no one is close enough to see my screen, knowing that what's contained in that message is likely filthy.

Upon opening the message, I inhale with a soft hiss. The text simply says, **Thinking of you.** With it, Gabby has sent a photo of her hand just at her entrance, as if she took the picture the moment she took her middle and ring finger out of herself. Those two fingers are covered in what I know can only be her slick. I take another deep swig of water, gulping it down in an attempt to quell the rising heat in my core.

Looks like you're doing a little more than thinking, I reply.

Right away, the little speech bubble pops up toward the bottom of my screen to indicate Gabby or Darius is typing.

It's a message from Darius that pops up on my screen next. **Is the jammer an expert on jamming things? Or on jam itself? We have a lot to learn if we're going to be in shape for Hairy Pitts in a couple weeks. Wouldn't want to embarrass you.**

A broad smile overtakes my face. I couldn't help it even if I wanted to. The anxiety in my body alchemizes into gleeful jitters as I type my reply. **I think you're more than familiar with my ability to jam things in my mouth and jam fingers into handy places.** I add an eye-rolling emoji, then continue: **But as you might expect, I never say no to homemade jam... in case you're offering, Chef.**

Darius replies with a devilish grin emoji and this: **I seem to recall**

at least one other part of your body that can take a good jamming.

I roll my eyes and feel my face go sanguine. I send a gif of an animated purple face sticking their tongue out and one word in reply: **Smartass.**

I give myself a shake and decide to burn off this energy on the track, putting my mouth guard back in and skating towards my friends, absolutely giddy and ready to kick their asses.

At work the next day, I could cut the sexual tension between Gabby and me with the box cutter I carry holstered at my hip. The anticipation of spending an entire weekend sharing a big bed with Gabby and Darius is enough to drive me wild.

Gabby and I find ourselves pulling product for my section together. Our breath seems to touch between us, the clouds colliding in the freezer. Gabby's eyes have that hungry look that is becoming so deliciously familiar to me, and they hit me like an elbow to the gut. She plants a hasty, sloppy kiss on me and I push her gently towards the door to ensure no one can surprise us coming in. Quickly, I lift her shirt and she lets out a soft gasp of surprise, a smile and a hint of nervousness playing across her face. "I just want a quick taste," I explain. She nods.

I yank down the blue cotton bralette she has on unceremoniously and affix my lips around one of her nipples, then the other, sucking softly and swirling my tongue around their hardness. She pants and gasps again as the freezing air meets my spit on her skin. I have a split second to take her in— back against the door, tits in the air, nipples glossy with my kisses— before she hastily tucks herself back into her bra, then her shirt back into her pants.

We finish pulling what we need to replenish the stock outside quickly enough, but we're quiet for the rest of our shift together, and I know why. The desire has silenced us. All we can do is want and fantasize and yearn and burn until we can touch again.

Darius and Gabby invite me to ride with them out to Harrisburg. Normally, I ride with Dee on trips like this, but we talked about it and she said it would be a good chance for me to bond with them and tell them the truth about Ollie and the breakup. I don't know why she's so worried. I'll sort it out eventually. I can't think about that too hard right now. I have the most important derby tournament of the season just ahead of me, not to mention what I anticipate to be Olympic-level sex. Not in the competitive sense, but in the level of skill, dedication, and I'm hoping, endurance.

I am hoping this trip will offer us some quality bonding time too, though. I'm weirdly looking forward to doing something as mundane as sitting in the car for three hours together. Being on a derby team that occasionally travels for the past few years, I know all too well how much you can learn about people when crammed into a vehicle with them for hours on end.

I know that we haven't promised each other anything, but while I've been unsure whether I should put myself back out there, I accidentally found myself already there. How did a kinky sex site meetup turn into a weekend away together, and is there potential for more? Do I *want* more? I must at least be curious, if I invited them. I'm unsettled by how unsure of my own motivations I am. This is totally uncharted territory.

But, I haven't thought of Alan almost at all since meeting them. My missing Ollie has only grown, though, as well as my sense of betrayal, which I've been trying to keep at arm's length at all costs. The longing isn't for Alan and Ollie as a package deal any longer, for the little family and home we made together. *I just miss my dog and want to move on.* Was that little voice the same one that told me to leave Ollie behind? That the three of us belonged together? I hope Gabby and Darius make me come hard enough to get me out of my own head before my first bout.

We're in Gabby's beat-up white sedan, the car surprisingly well taken care of on the inside, save for the odd stain on its tan, leather interior.

Gabby insisted on driving and Darius said he wanted to feel like he was being chauffeured, so he's taken up the backseat. I'm in the trusted co-pilot and car DJ seat and fully letting the power go to my head, playing all my favorite road trip tunes. Gabby and I learn that we have quite a wide Venn diagram center of common ground in our music tastes, both of us favoring music that is fast with a good beat, regardless of genre. Occasionally, she requests a particular song, but mostly she seems happy to let me play DJ.

I get lost in conversation with the two of them and my shuffle takes over the music queue. A song comes on that instantly brings Alan to the forefront of my mind and I reach out to the control panel to skip it, but before I can push the button, Gabby says, "Aw, can you leave it?" The way she asks me in between singing along, as if she doesn't want to miss any of the lyrics, makes my heart melt a little. I let my hand drop back into my lap. During the instrumental bridge, Gabby says, "You don't like this song." It's a half-question, inviting me to explain. Darius says nothing from the backseat, but I know he's likely listening. He's been participating equally in our conversations.

"It reminds me of my ex," I say, unable to smooth the rasp in my voice.

Gabby groans. "Aw, why didn't you say so? I'm here screaming along like a freakin' banshee—"

"It's okay. It's actually nice," I cut Gabby off. "I feel like you're rewriting the memory for me. Plus, I can't run from my feelings forever. It's fine. It's a good song."

Gabby takes one hand off the steering wheel, grabs mine from my lap, and squeezes, the backs of her fingers brushing against my thigh as she does. I feel another hand, big and strong, squeeze my shoulder— Darius, reaching forward from the backseat.

"Fuck that guy," Darius says, and his voice is harsher than I've ever heard it. "I swear to God, just say the word and I will kidnap Ollie back for you."

Gabby sighs as she nods her head emphatically, releasing my hand and once again gripping the steering wheel. "Fuck that guy," she echoes.

"It wasn't all bad," I say softly. I can almost hear Dee's voice in my head: *Do it, bitch. Come clean. It's right there on the tip of your tongue. You can do it. Do the right thing, own your shit.*

Gabby glances my way, taking her eyes off the road for only a brief moment, and says, "I'm sure it wasn't. But it doesn't change that he betrayed your trust by keeping Ollie away from you. He's *your* dog, and just because you dumped him doesn't give him the right to behave like an asshole."

The words hit me with the force of a ton of bricks, a massive pyramid impossibly sharpened to a dagger-point, right in the chest. "I'm the asshole," I manage to say out loud. Dee's voice boomerangs back through my mind. *You're so close, bitch. Tell. The. Truth.*

"Hey," Darius says, his tone serious, but the sharp ice from before now gone. I turn around as much as I can in my seat to face him. "You're *not* an asshole. Broken hearts hurt, but you leaving him doesn't make you responsible for his fucked-up way of dealing with it. *Especially* not when he's hurting you with his so-called coping."

The two-ton force of the dagger in my chest doubles. I can't. I can't possibly tell the truth. *I'm* the one with the fucked-up coping mechanisms. *I'm* the liar. The manipulator. I face forward again and shake my head. "You're right," I say, and lean my forehead against the window to watch the Pennsylvania countryside roll by. I hope the angle is enough to hide the tears I can't help from rolling down my cheeks.

 **29**

Darius' Hairy Pitts

When we get to the hotel, I'm worried. After that whole exchange about her ex in the car, Vic hardly said a word the rest of the way here. We hadn't even made it to Harrisburg and the awkward implosion I was desperately hoping against... happened. Gabby usually is pretty adept at diffusing these kinds of situations, but even she has remained somber and quiet for the past hour.

Vic unlocks the door to our hotel room with her keycard, then holds the door open for Gabby and me to walk in.

Vic immediately heads into the bathroom and shuts the door. Gabby heads for the stiff-looking orange couch against the wall in the middle of the room, and I stand by the door taking it all in. There really isn't much to take in. On my right is the bathroom door Vic just went through. On my left is an above-average hotel kitchenette with a full-sized fridge and a full set of plates and glasses neatly shelved above the sink, on either side of the microwave.

Gabby now sits on the orange couch, her feet propped up on a matching ottoman. It, along with a scuffed-up laminate wood coffee table, sit atop a hideous striped rug that reminds me of old desktop screensavers.

"This unimpressive hotel sure does bring back a lot of *great* memories," I say in a stilted, cheesy voice, laying it on thick and projecting enough to know Vic can hear me in the bathroom, even with the fan on.

Gabby says, "Smooth. Is this the kind of quick, on-your-feet thinking you're learning in improv class?"

"It sure is making me immune to embarrassment and making a fool of myself," I say, not breaking the overdone, cheesy voice.

Suddenly, Vic opens the bathroom door and steps past me swiftly. "What is this bit? If you can even call it that. What's with the voice?" She clears the space to the bed in a few brisk steps and flops onto the fluffy duvet and down pillows. I walk over to the desk on the left side of the room, tug the rolling chair from its tucked-in spot at the desk against the wall, and sit, facing Gabby and Vic on the other sides of the room, the three of us forming a triangle.

I shrug, smiling smugly at Vic, though her face is turned away. "Got you to talk." My eyes dart to Gabby, whose eyes are wide with concern, but I can tell she's trying to keep her emotions in check, trying not to freak out. I turn my attention back to Vic. "Do you *want* to talk? About whatever is bothering you?"

"I'm fine," Vic says, the two monosyllabic words seeming to come out clipped even shorter.

"Well, it's obvious you're upset about the ex-boyfriend conversation we had in the car," I press.

"No, serious—"

I cut Vic off before she can continue with whatever protest she was about to insist upon. "Fine. Forget the whole thing. We're here for *you*." I flail my hand around, emphatically gesturing back and forth between me and Gabby. "We wanted to come out here and see what you do, play cheerleader, have some fun together. Let's just start over."

Vic turns her head and considers me for a long moment, until I see a tentative smile tug at the corners of her pink mouth. "Are you gonna wear tiny cheer shorts for me? Maybe even a pleated mini skirt?"

"If you want me to," I say, and my smile is dead serious.

"Good idea, babe. Fresh start." Gabby lets out a whoosh of air.

"I could eat," Vic says.

We end up at a local pub where it somehow comforts me that the buns taste like dry tissue paper. I'm a chef, but I ate a lot of trash as a teenage boy and young rogue in culinary school. A lot of it was good trash, but a good bit of it wasn't, especially in the fake ID years. Shitty burgers like this take me back to that fond, regrettable time.

The fries aren't half bad, though, hot and glistening. I dunk them in ketchup and shove them in my mouth in spindly, spudly clusters. I playfully swat away Gabby's and Vic's hands as they pilfer them off my plate, wishing I had gotten the chicken tenders they ordered instead of my sad burger.

Sub-par meal aside, my heart melts into my stomach as I watch the two of them giggling, listen to them bond over their favorite

TV shows and talking shit about annoying customers at work. I feel a surge of protectiveness toward Vic, wanting to keep her like this, smiling and laughing, for as long as possible. I hated seeing her sad and withdrawn earlier. I hate the person who made her feel that way, that jerk.

I've never cared about anyone like this, except Gabby. I genuinely never thought I would find this feeling inside me for anyone but her. Sure, I'm a classic introvert, I'm an anxious guy who takes some time to process emotions. But whatever it is, nameless though it may be for now, I feel something stirring in my chest for Vic, for the way she fits into my life, into *our* lives.

While we're waiting for the check, Vic gets a text from Dee, her best friend. She told us a bit about her favorite people on the team towards the beginning of our roadtrip. Most of the names and details have blurred and smudged in my mind, but Dee stood out as her best friend and coworker. Gabby enthusiastically shared that she is also very much a fan of Dee. Apparently the whole closing crew is "legendary" and Dee can break down pallets like nobody's business— "even ones that are loaded up with heavy cases of sparkling water and falling over," Gabby said, eyes wide and head bobbing for emphasis as she drove.

Apparently, the text from Dee is an invitation for the three of us to join the team at a bar that doesn't seem too far from us, according to the GPS app. We decide to walk over to take in the city. Not much is open, in fact, a lot of the downtown area seems to be made up of abandoned buildings. It's my first time here in Harrisburg; it reminds me of Pittsburgh, the distinct rusty flavor of a town that used to be as strong as the steel it produced.

Gabby slips her arm into mine, and as I look over to her, I see that on her other side, she holds Vic's hand, too. I feel a zap in my chest, as if there is truly a current running between the three of us, along the line of our skins' mutual touch. Walking like this along the sidewalk together, side by side, we barely fit. It doesn't matter. There's hardly another soul out here. It's quiet, it's romantic.

We get to the bar: "Eleanor's," which has a caricature of Eleanor Roosevelt presiding over the joint, painted on a back wall above the hallway to the bathrooms.

An hour into hanging out with Vic's friends, I feel like Larry David in *Curb Your Enthusiasm*. "Lesbians love me!" Well, sapphics and punky riot grrrl derby bitches apparently do, and I mean that in the most badass way possible.

Vic's derby friends are intense and warm and lovely to be around. Some of them are more outspoken and outgoing than others, but none of them make me feel pressured to engage, and weirdly, though I'm one of only three men in our group (some of the other women brought along their guy partners as well), I don't feel out of place at all.

After about an hour of us hanging out at the bar, someone unexpectedly starts singing karaoke in the corner, on a machine I hadn't noticed when we walked in. Almost the entire team shrieks in excitement as the first digitally rendered notes of "I Will Survive" start up and the woman in the corner leans into the dramatic pauses of the first verse. Next thing I know, Gabby and Vic are up there hollering their way through "Girls Just Wanna Have Fun," and I find myself pulled to the "stage" area by some of the women to join in on a numetal classic when they catch me singing along from the table.

Back at the hotel, we're pooped from being on the road all day and our little night on the town. I take a quick shower, then Gabby and Vic decide to shower together. I scroll on my phone and wait for them to come to bed, taking the side closest to the door.

I watch as the two of them emerge wrapped in their towels to change into comfy night clothes, Gabby in just a loosely fitting vintage band tee, Vic in a coordinating purple pajama set. It's not sexual, but it feels intimate in the extreme. They're quiet, going through the motions of their nighttime routines and rummaging through drawers and bags.

I gulp my heart down from my throat back into my aching chest, the warm everydayness of this moment too much for me to handle, the feeling of everything locking into place, being as it should. *As it should?* I push away the cold nip of guilt that threatens to ruin the moment. *Gabby has always been enough for me.* Still, it's not that she's not enough... It's just that being here, together with Vic, feels so *right,* instinctive, as Gabby had put it. I decide it's best just to enjoy the moment and not think about it too hard. It's nice. Can't it just be a nice weekend together without me dissecting the whole experience for larger meaning?

They crawl into bed beside me, Vic in between us, Gabby by the window.

It takes us a few minutes to settle into comfortable positions. I end up spooning Vic, she and Gabby face each other, Vic running her hand across Gabby's dark hair in smooth, soothing strokes. "We call this forking," Gabby informs Vic with a smile, referring to the spooning inverse position the two of them are in together currently, their legs twining together like the tines of two forks.

"Goodnight you two," I say.

"Sweet dreams," Gabby says.

"Don't let the bed bugs bite," says Vic.

I sleep peacefully that night, waking up only once from the overwhelming body heat the three of us generate under the massive duvet. I slip back into sleep easily, one leg exposed to the air and wrapped around Vic. She sleeps soundly beside me, arm wrapped around Gabby who is now in the littlest spoon position, facing the window, the duvet rising and falling with her deep, even breaths.

"This is nice," I sigh into the drowsy dark.

30

Vic's Hairy Pitts

My alarm goes off at 8 am. It's an obnoxiously loud blaring sound that makes me think of toxic disasters. I'm a heavy sleeper who loves to hit the snooze button and this is the only sound that helps me wake up successfully.

"Holy hell," Darius groans from beside me. "Please, make it stop." He hands me my phone from the nightstand beside him.

Gabby echoes the sentiment with a wordless groan. I quickly tap my screen to stop the torture.

We eat breakfast at the high-top tables in the corporate-looking gray hotel lobby punctuated by the most atrocious combination of accent colors: grey-blue, orange, and a soulless shade of green that looks like it came pre-faded. The food isn't bad and a good number of the Barbedbies are down here eating, too. Many of them chatter and laugh despite the early hour.

"You're quiet," Gabby says.

I nod. "I always get the jitters before a bout. This is going to go right through me," I say, gesturing with the breakfast sandwich in my hands. It's a sausage egg and cheese with buns made of waffles. I take a swig of my coffee, which Darius made for me. Light and sweet, just how I like it. *He remembered.*

Darius and Gabby both nod as if the information I just shared about my nervous bowel movements is the most normal tidbit to divulge over breakfast. It strikes me that with these two, maybe it is. I don't have to hide from them or pretend. A pang of guilt threatens to ruin my appetite, and I take a huge bite of my sandwich in an effort to suppress the shame before it can consume me. I can feel shitty about my lies and deception later, and maybe, just maybe, try to make things right. If Gabby and Darius will still have me. Today, my girls are counting on me.

After I use the bathroom, I throw myself on the bed beside Darius, who is scrolling absentmindedly on his phone. Gabby is doing the same, but she is sprawled on the orange loveseat, soft pop music emanating from her phone. I snuggle into Darius, burying myself into his side, the slight musk of his underarm comforting me as I rest my head on his chest. "The bout isn't until 4. What are you gonna do until then?" he asks me.

I sigh, trying to shake off some of my nerves and lean into the contented feeling washing over me from his closeness. "A nap sounds pretty good right about now. I have to be at the track at one to help set up, take pictures, warm up. All that crap."

Over Darius' chest, I watch Gabby rise to her feet. She stretches and groans into the movement, wiggling her fingers as if she could reach the ceiling if she really tried. "A nap sounds *divine,* darling," she drawls in a silly posh accent.

"Was that supposed to be British?" I heckle.

She shrugs and gives me a big, playful smile. "I was going more for that like, Grace Kelly/Audrey Hepburn Mid-Atlantic thing."

I groan my disapproval. "Oh boy, you should have just lied and let me think my British guess was right."

She flops onto the bed beside me, the same spot she occupied last night. I turn to face her, and Darius shifts in the same direction, bracketing me into him with one arm around my waist.

"After we nap, would you do my eye makeup for me?" I ask Gabby.

Her eyes almost seem to shimmer with excitement. "You would trust me to do your big game-day makeup?"

"It's called a bout, babe," Darius says, but the words are muffled as he's speaking them into my hair. I felt him breathing me in a moment before, his nose pressed against the back of my head as if he can't get enough of my scent.

"Whatever," Gabby says.

"Of course I trust you," I say in answer to Gabby's initial question, and my words come out more earnest than I'd intended, as if there's a deeper layer of meaning beyond eyeshadow palettes and the ten types of face glitter currently stuffed in my makeup bag in the hotel bathroom. I add, "I have a routine for the rest of my face, but I've seen the magic you work on your occasional 'get-ready-with-me' videos."

"Oh, you've seen me work my magic in *all* kinds of videos," she purrs, turning to face the window and settling against me, her ass pressed into me, my ass pressed into Darius. "I'd be honored to do your eyes, babe," she says, yawning.

Babe. That's the first time either of them have called me something other than my name outside of a sexual context. I let sleep wash over me as I listen to the intermingled sounds of our breathing.

I wake to gentle light filtering through the sheer hotel curtain, and to even gentler caresses from both Darius and Gabby that turn into us fucking languidly, tenderly, for the moment, my nerves completely forgotten. Afterward, Gabby and I take another shower together. I put on my uniform tank, fishnets, and signature sparkly purple booty shorts with the unicorn patch I embroidered on with less-than-expert skill. I think the shitty job I did attaching the patch makes it look more punk. That's what I tell myself, anyway.

I sit on the orange couch as Gabby rolls herself over to me on the chair that was tucked under the hotel room desk. As she does, I hear the shower start running again and Darius' low, off-key humming over the sound of spraying water. My two makeup bags and three eyeshadow palettes sit beside me, sinking slightly into the space between the couch cushions because of my weight pressing into the couch.

Gabby studies each palette briefly, a look of rather serious concentration settling over her sweet features. She stacks the third and final palette onto the other two, which she has now placed on the ottoman beside her. She clasps her hands across her knee, one leg crossed over the other. "So what look are we going for? Sexy, intimidating badass bitch? 'I-love-rainbows-and-unicorns-but-I-will-fuck-you-up?' Purple with a dash of purple and some purple to finish it off?" Her brows do a little jig above her eyes and I chuckle.

"All of the above?" I say, my words sounding more like a question. "Do your worst."

"A little faith, please," she says, leaning forward to grab my makeup bags from beside me, her hand brushing my thigh as she does.

She prepares my eyelids for the shadow and her movements are gentle as she pats concealer onto my lids, setting it with powder at the end of a fluffy brush. She's so close to me that I feel her breath on my closed eyelids and the moment is so overwhelmingly sweet I feel like something inside me breaks.

Gabby instructs me to open, close, open, close my eyes as she applies the shadow, and I obey. She blows on my lids after applying liquid liner and I try not to give into the flutter the sensation triggers. Finally, she rummages through the pouch with (a portion of) my glitter collection, letting out gleeful oohs and ahhs as her fingers search through them all, the little plastic pots clacking pleasantly against each other as she does. Finally, she chooses an electric blue, ultra-fine glitter. "Blue?" I say, letting my surprise show in my voice.

"Trust me," she says, and this time I wonder if I hear my own earnestness from earlier echoing back at me, wonder if there's a deeper intention imbued into those two words. Gabby swipes the pad of her finger into the glitter gel and orders me in an almost-whisper to close my eyes again. She presses her finger gently onto my lids and the shower stops. "Take a look," she says after about 30 seconds of blowing on me to ensure the glitter set properly.

I turn my head to the left and catch my first glimpse of myself in the big mirror. Even from a few feet away, the look Gabby has given me is high drama, which means it will play well on the track. I stand and walk over to the mirror to get a better look at her handiwork. The wings she painted at either outer corner of my eyes are perfectly even, thick and sharp as knives. The best part is the bright blue glitter she picked. Against the broody purple shades she used to paint my lids, it creates an effect almost like stars glittering at dusk, though I've never seen a sky as magical as this.

"I love it! Thank you, Gabby." I smile at her, our eyes meeting in our reflections in the mirror. She closes the distance between us and hugs me from behind, then plants a big kiss on my cheek.

Darius comes out of the bathroom. He starts getting dressed and Gabby gets herself together as well, as I start in on the rest of my usual makeup routine. The whole scene feels so normal, it's poetic. It feels like it was always meant to be this way.

When Darius and Gabby ask if they can come help set up at the track, I eye them suspiciously.

"Don't you want to explore town a bit? Relax in the hotel? Why would you volunteer to carry a bunch of fold-out tables and chairs and be bossed around by a bunch of furies?"

Darius is quick to say, "Well, you *know* I like that last part." He winks goofily. Gabby adds, "We came to support, remember? We're happy to do more than just cheer you on from the stands, especially if we can actually help make your day less stressful."

My heart lurches in my chest. I've lost count at the number of times it's done that this weekend, but that doesn't make it any less uncomfortable now. I tell myself that's just Gabby. She'd offer the same to any of her friends, hell, even a stranger.

We arrive at the track and I lose Gabby and Darius almost immediately, Dee barking orders at them from across the building.

The track where Hairy Pitts is being held this year— and where the local derby team practices— is, at its most basic, a massive warehouse. Over the years, (renter friendly-ish) modifications have been made to spruce up the place and make it the derby hub of the Pennsylvania capitol. I have no clue how we would disassemble and remove the several-ton monstrosity that is the concession stand, made of salvaged and repurposed vintage cars—much of it welded together— but I'm sure we could figure it out if the landlords decided they'd had enough of our pinup/rockabilly/punk Barbarella nonsense.

Both teams are present, socializing with friendly familiarity as they go about their tasks. I notice some of the women decorating, so I join in. It's my favorite task at these sorts of events, and I'm good at it. We blow balloons and fill a massive net with them. Somebody apparently knows how to rig this thing to the ceiling for a balloon drop at the end of the awards ceremony. When Rosalind starts mentioning the cherry picker they'll need to use and the lock they'll need to pick to get to the keys for it, I plug my ears with my index fingers and shout "plausible deniability" over and over until they shut up.

The decorating team moves to put up some signage so the gawking masses know where to go. At this point, Gabby and

Darius finish with Dee and join my group. In the five minutes this final task takes, I learn they were setting up some tables around the venue— some for merch, some for security to check bags, and a few others.

"I honestly don't know what you all would have done without me here," Darius tells me, voice dripping with sarcasm. We walk toward where everyone is standing by the track, done with our duties and gravitating naturally toward the group without being directed. I roll my eyes.

Dee jogs by from seemingly out of nowhere and punches him in the arm, apparently having heard his pseudo-macho comment.

When we reach the group, Rosalind announces, "Alright, bitches. Get purdy! You're all lookin' a little sweaty right now and it's..." She glances at her smart watch, which has a spiked band. "Forty-five minutes till showtime," she finishes.

In the locker room, it's the usual crowded flurry of skates and braids and glitter, fishnets and tights in every color. I lean in close to a full-length mirror on the wall to wipe under my eyes, wanting Gabby's masterpiece to remain as perfect as she envisioned it.

A little while later, as we stand in two close lines to take our Hairy Pitts team photo, I see Gabby and Darius looking on, half-watching the photo session as they chat with other partners and loved ones of my teammates. The crowd is filtering in steadily now, the big space filling with sound. A funny feeling takes up residence in my chest, like a nervous squirrel is skittering up and down my ribcage.

Alan was always good at these things. He was social, most of my team liked him. Hell, most of the league liked him. As I glance at Darius and Gabby between camera clicks, I notice that while Darius is certainly engaged, Gabby is a lot more in her element. I catch Darius' face lighting up when he thinks of a silly comment just for her ears— I can almost see his "improv brain" light turn on.

The little woodland creature in my chest seems to be satisfied that this tree is safe for now.

As I glide up the wall of the raised track to take my position as starting jammer for my team, I can't see Gabby and Darius in the crowd. In fact, I don't take in much of anything when I'm getting my head in the game for a bout. My mind naturally tunnels in on the action, blocking out sounds and zeroing in visually on the track, my team, my opponents, the crowd outside the chainlink fence that walls the raised track. Knowing they're there, though, something washes over me, like herbal tea filling my bones and soothing my nerves.

I'm vaguely aware that the Spinsters, the team we're facing, decided to use Rhonda as their starting jammer. In my periphery, I see her elbows form almost identical "Ls" to mine as she takes her position. I imagine the two of us from an outsider's perspective, almost seeming suspended as we stand perfectly still, muscles tense with anticipation. We fix our gazes straight ahead of us as our teams blast forward at the sound of the first whistle. My heartbeat thunks loudly in my star-marked helmet as I wait the eternal few moments for the second whistle that serves as the signal for me to skate my ass off.

Just when I think I'll go mad from chomping at the bit, my whistle sounds. I don't tell my body to move, it just does, responding to the whistle by second nature.

For the first few strokes of movement, Rhonda's skates and mine clatter along the track in almost-perfect unison. I scramble to propel myself forward, the familiar feeling of flinging my body through space on wheels taking over all other sensations. The gravity of my limbs comes down, pushing me forward, forward, my wheels an extension of my body. With a few more strides, I make it past the Spinster at the back of the pack. One of my teammates reaches toward me in invitation, but before I can raise my arm even halfway to meet her outstretched hand, a Spinster comes up at four o' clock and hip checks her, sending my teammate to a skid on her padded hands and knees, foiling her attempt to whip me forward before we can even start.

I refocus my attention on making it through the pack of derby babes. I need to get to the other side of them and make my way fully around the track so I can start going about getting what I came here to do: Win.

Rhonda makes it through before I do, and the sight of her skating clear of my teammates, nothing but open track ahead of her, has me spitting out a curse. By the time I make it past the last Spinster, dodging a blow from her elbow, Rhonda's halfway around the track. Shit. Just like that, I spend the first half of the bout playing catch-up.

I'm able to score some points, but Marnie has Dee jam after I fall in a skidding bellyflop on the track for the second time, then puts in Tracy. At halftime, the Spinsters have a firm lead, the score 32 to 20.

The second half is better, my defensive skills proving to be a lot more valuable than my jamming skills today, but we still lose the bout—and the whole Hairy Pitts shebang— by an infuriating three points.

We good-game high-five the Spinsters and skate into the locker room, a familiar bittersweetness edged with playful, self-deprecating disappointment among us more veteran derby girls. The rookies among us look like they want to punch and scream and cry the rest of the day away. I clap my arm around Veronica, as we skate stiffly over to the locker room. "I know it sucks," I tell her. "I was you not that long ago."

She looks at me incredulously, some of the anger at the bout's outcome heating its way through her gaze, now directed at me. "Don't you care that we lost?" she accuses, the last word coming out almost as sharp as a hiss.

I shrug. "Yeah, of course I care. In fact, in some ways having won past Hairy Pitts makes losing harder, because I know we can do it."

"Okay then?" Veronica's brow squiggles with confusion as she shrugs out of my side-hug.

"Having won before gives me enough hope, I guess. The experience tells me that 'there's always next time,'" — I air-quote— "is actually true. I'm confident I did my best. I'm confident *we* did our best. We just didn't take it all this time."

The expression in Veronica's eyes cools slightly, the corner of her mouth pulling into an almost-smile.

My own eyes prick at my words, as if I've cast a spell on myself, the feeling of delayed realization taking me by surprise like a gust of cold air as I change in the locker room, only half-aware of the post-bout small talk I'm involved in.

I walk out of the locker room with my duffle slung over a shoulder, my knees protesting at every step from the beatings I took on the track. Focusing on taking small steps, I stare at the ground trying not to get lost in thought, until I feel eyes on me and lift my gaze from the ground to see Gabby and Darius each holding half of a massive lavender poster-board sign with royal-worthy purple glitter letters that glint and wink at me in perfect script to spell "VICIOUS VULVA." I know the letters must be Darius' doing, the work of a practiced, even hand. There's also a gloopy thing made of glitter gel above the words that I think is supposed to be a leaping unicorn, clearly a freehanded Gabby specialty. They must have brought the sign with them from Pittsburgh and hidden it somewhere in the trunk of Gabby's car so that I wouldn't see it. Bouncing from the sign, my gaze meets Gabby's, then Darius' eyes, which seem to be shining with something I've never seen them direct at me... Is it pride?

My chest clenches around my heart in response to the way they're looking at me, confirming what my advice to Veronica caused to unexpectedly bubble up a few minutes ago: *I'm in love with them.*

All that talk about winning and losing, how losing one match makes the winning all the sweeter, how losing can't take anything away from our wins... I let the "loss" of Alan, the perceived "failure" of our relationship, close me off from hope for another deep connection, meanwhile, the universe hands me not one but *two* incredible people on a deliciously hedonistic platter. That is, if they'll have me.

Gabby and Darius were initially very clear about their relationship boundaries. We're just supposed to be friends with benefits, nothing more. But they made that boundary when we were nothing more than strangers, when we were just Food Freaxxx to each other. That was before all the mind-blowing sex, before getting to know each other. Before our one-on-one time together, sleepovers, countless meals and showers and streaming our favorite shows on the couch. It was before they offered to drive me to Hairy Pitts, before they spent the weekend away with me getting to know my friends, before they came all this way just to cheer me on and made me a sign... Before they looked at me *like that.*

I reach the spot where they're standing and they pull me into a group hug, Darius taking my duffle and switching it over to his own shoulder as he pulls away. Okay, I love them. How the hell am I going to tell them? If I tell them the truth about my feelings, I will finally have to come clean about everything. And if I do that, they will surely cut me out of their lives. I know trust is important to them, and I've broken their trust before they've even fully given it to me. Suddenly, my whole being aches in a way that goes much deeper than any of my derby bruises.

A future I hadn't realized I'd imagined— hadn't realized I'd been *yearning* for— starts to slip away, sinking from my vision: my future with Gabby and Darius. *When did I start to see myself* with *them?* Shit.

I'm in love with Gabby and Darius. And I fucked it all up before it even had a chance to start.

227

31

Darius' Churning

When I wake up this morning, back in the bed I share with Gabby after dropping Vic off at her place last night, all the tangled threads in my head seem to be neatly wound on their spools and organized by color in ROYGBIV order. I sigh with relief at the clarity I've finally achieved, mingled with frustration at my process of figuring out my thoughts and feelings.

What is the clarity in my head telling me? Monogamy and I are over.

That is, if Gabby is on board.

Technically, we're not even really monogamous anymore. We're having threesomes with Vic left and right, we hang out with her all the time. It all feels so... *normal.*

Is this about Vic? I wonder to myself. Clear as a bell, I hear myself respond, *Not for me.* But maybe it is for Gabby. Does Gabby want Vic to be her girlfriend? *Our* girlfriend? Equally important, is that something Vic would want? Can I see myself as her boyfriend? Partner? I mean, the sex is great, it's fun, I don't want it to end, but I don't know if I could ever form a connection with someone else as deep as the one Gab and I share. The clear, calm feeling inside me says, *I already have.*

At work, I spend the day distracted, reading on my breaks about different types of non-monogamy: Kitchen table polyamory, open relationships with varying rules and levels of balance... Maybe I should have done this when Gabby first proposed the threesome, but I never thought things would get this far. By the end of the day, I have a headache from all the information I've attempted to take in, and apparently I wasn't doing my best work. A customer called to complain that I mistakenly piped a plain "Happy Birthday" on their cake. They had requested "Hippie Birthday, Maaan" on their custom form. I also forgot to pipe the peace sign they had requested. Rebecca had to refund them.

"What's with you?" she asks me once we've closed for the day. I join her out in the parking lot, both of us leaning on her car as she smokes a cigarette. They don't bother me. They're nostalgic for me, they remind me of my dad and his friends back home in Miami. A bunch of chain-smoking loud mouths whose idea of affection is a too-rough noogie. I should call.

I sigh in response to Rebecca's question. I share about my personal life occasionally with her, but it's just not in my nature to trust easily, and I feel awkward bringing up what's on my mind. We've known each other for a long time, and we're friends, but she's still my coworker.

Despite myself, I feel my mouth forming the words I wasn't sure I could say out loud. "I think I want to talk to Gabby about us being non-monogamous." My voice sounds tight. Why is there a lump in my throat?

"Oh, shit." Rebecca blinks hard, then her eyes go wide, as if she's making sure she heard me correctly. She ashes her cigarette on the asphalt. She's talking fast now. "Are things good, though? Are you unhappy? You guys have been together *forever*."

"I'm deliriously happy. I want to be with her *actually* forever." I shrug. "I don't know. Nothing's wrong. I just *know* it's something I want, or at least want to try."

"Did this just come out of nowhere?" Rebecca asks.

"No," I answer flatly.

"Care to elaborate?"

I raise my eyebrows as if to say, "Don't push it."

"No? Okay. Well, I don't need to tell you what to do. I think you already know," Rebecca says.

I run my hand across my buzzed head and sigh again. "Yeah, I need to talk to her. Thanks for listening. Don't get used to me spilling my guts to you. I'm gonna go catch my bus."

"I can give you a ride," Rebecca offers.

"Nah, I'm a creature of habit," I say, not wanting to be rude and confess that I just want to be alone, albeit on a bus full of strangers. I find comfort in the anonymity.

Rebecca smiles and I ruffle her hair. She slaps my hand away and I start across the parking lot to my bus stop. Then, as I wait for the bus, she drives by and shouts, "Good luck!" out the window.

Walking into the apartment, something smells amazing. "What's cookin', good lookin'?" I grab Gabby from behind as she sautés something at our stove. She worked an earlier shift today, and it's nice having her home for dinnertime.

"Picadillo," she says, and leans her head back for a kiss, pressing her ass playfully into my pelvis, a triple-threat of multi-tasking as she keeps moving the spatula among the cumin-blasted ground beef, onions, peppers, and olives of her abuela's classic recipe.

"Raisins this time?" I ask. Sometimes she's in the mood to add them to the picadillo, sometimes not. Most people find the olive and raisin debate polarizing; Gabby just goes with whichever she's in the mood for that particular day.

I take the big wooden spoon from the spoon rest and give the rice a mindless stir. The rice seems to be just about ready, but it will probably be a little mushy. I smile. Gabby always prefers for me to make the rice because I have what she calls the "special touch" for it. I estimate that she didn't want to ask me to do it after the long day she knows I've had, still in the final throes of our busy wedding season.

"No raisins today," she answers.

I shower, we eat and watch something together as we do. I'm too out of it to follow the episode and barely respond to Gabby's commentary.

Talking to Gabby about wanting to explore casual connections with other people, especially men, independently was entirely painless. After everything we've been through with Vic, it's old hat. Was it really only a few months ago that I thought our relationship would be ruined by having a threesome? It seems like a lifetime ago. Gab was understanding and supportive of my latest explorative interest.

One key difference in my latest venture, though, is that finding a man to hook up with was ridiculously easy compared to finding a bisexual woman to hook up with the two of us. I guess that's why people like Vic get labeled "unicorns," so rare and precious are they.

Within literal minutes of downloading a gay hookup app, creating my profile, and toggling my search settings, I had more than a handful of horny, explicit messages pouring into my inbox on the app. A couple of them ghosted me almost right away, others seemed nice enough, but one was willing to meet tonight.

After checking in with Gabby one more time to make sure this wasn't all happening too fast, I made plans to meet this stranger. All I know about him is that he loves sloppy blowjobs and he has a nice cock.

It's not a far walk to @biking_bi_king's apartment. On the way, I'm semi-hard and full of jitters. My thoughts are coming at me fast. My mouth feels dry, I find myself stumbling over little uneven sections of sidewalk. On a loop, I think to myself, *Why am I nervous?* then, *It's normal to be nervous.* Neither of these thoughts calms my nerves.

Suddenly, I'm punching in the number he messaged me on the box outside his apartment building and he's buzzing me in.

We sit on the edge of his bed, we kiss, our pants come off. My cock is hard and in his mouth in minutes. @biking_bi_king is on his knees now and my mind goes blank except there's a new loop on repeat, this time aloud: "Oh, fuck."

Until Vic, Gabby was the only person who had ever given me a blowjob, and her blowjobs are absolutely legendary (to me). They're amazing. Somewhere in the back of my mind, I think that it's nice to experience something new, something different. @biking_bi_king has a blowjob style unique to him, and I would find it really beautiful if I weren't in mind-numbing himbo ecstasy.

"I want to taste you, too," I finally manage to whisper. I don't know why I'm whispering.

After a few more hungry gulps of my cock, @biking_bi_king releases me, looks up and smiles naughtily.

"You want a taste of me? Sucking you has me hard and dripping," he says, then he stands up and pushes me onto my back on the bed. He jerks his chin in an upward motion to let me know he wants me further back on the bed. "How about if I ride your face?" he says.

"Mmm, yes please," I answer without hesitation. My sexy stranger gracefully squats with one leg on either side of my face, using the headboard for balance by grabbing it with one hand. "So strong," I tease. He smiles, then he holds the tip of his cock to my lips. I lick the salty pre-cum off the tip and it sets off a wild, hungry growl from the back of my throat. I wrap my lips around his cock to signal I'm ready for him, and he slips it into my mouth, moving his hips gently at first, then fully humping my face in an animalistic way that sends me to a place I can only describe as bliss.

I moan around his cock, which is covered with my slobber. He grunts and moans, and I find myself loving the vulgar baritone harmony we create together, delightfully new music to me. The scene is too fucking hot for me not to touch myself, so I grab a fistful of my own hard length and pump it while he rides my face.

Finally, I'm exhausted and need to take a breather from getting face-fucked into oblivion, tears forming at the corners of my eyes. I tap him on his ass to let him know I need a break, and as he slips out of my mouth, I find myself missing him already.

"Whew, my thighs are gonna be burning tomorrow," he says, wiping his brow with his forearm. He glistens with sex sweat, we chuckle, and the sound of our voices laughing together is a lovely contrast to the filth we're getting up to.

His laugh peters out into a pleasure-filled sigh, and now my cock is in his mouth again, his cute, round ass in the air next to me. I smack it softly, playfully, then hold onto it for dear life as he sucks my soul out of my body.

Sitting back against the headboard beside me, he spits my come out onto his cock in a slow stream that makes the world itself slow its turn, then licks his lips slowly, savoring me. "Stroke me?" he asks, eyes pleading, voracious. I grab his cock again and lean in to kiss him. He's hard and sticky-wet. The sound it makes as I jerk him off is so delectable it makes my own cock ache. Our kisses are wet and passionate. His voice breathy and gruff against my mouth, he asks, "Did you come good?"

"Oh yeah," I answer enthusiastically, electricity winding through me as the recent orgasm echoes in our words. "How does my come feel on your cock?" I ask in kind.

His breath catches. Another sweet slut who loves my dirty talk as much as I love to talk dirty. Perfect. "Are you going to come for me so your sweet come can mix with mine now? You're going to be such a sticky mess when I'm done with you. Do you like making a mess?"

"Uh-huh," he whimpers against my lips. He's stopped really kissing me now, just has his mouth open, tongue out in desperation, his moans reverberating deliciously in the close inches between our faces, wordlessly begging me for more. I can tell he's on the edge. In the back of my mind, I'm aware of how hot it is to have a complete stranger melt in my hands like this.

I tease him by licking his outstretched tongue. "You tasted so good, and you took my cock so good down your throat. You love gagging all over it, don't you?"

He nods mindlessly and I praise him in response, "Such a good cock slut. Such a good come slut." And with that master stroke of my voice and my grip, I feel sweet little drops of warm come hit the back of my hand.

He sputters and sighs, collapsing into me, resting his forehead in the crook of my neck.

We clean ourselves up, he offers me a beer, which I am glad to accept. He pats the spot next to him on the couch. "Do you like to cuddle?" he asks.

"Hell yeah, I like to cuddle!" I cozy up beside him and sip on my beer. We sit in the quiet, faint jazz in the background. I don't remember hearing it before, and I don't remember him turning it on. *Smooth*, I think to myself. "If I can ask... What's your name?" I say, my voice a little hoarse. In the musical quiet, I let my gaze widen and wander, taking in his living room.

"You can call me Al," he says, and I catch a glimpse of his gorgeous smile as I peer down at him.

"I'm Darius," I say.

"Okay," Al says neutrally.

The little white dog that greeted me when I arrived is sleeping, curled up in a perfect little donut shape in a doggie bed beside the couch where we're sitting.

"Your dog is the sweetest thing. Can I take a picture of it?"

"Him," he shares, then adds, "Sure."

I bend down and he perks up a little, his tail wagging shyly. "What's his name?" I ask, feeling an ease between us.

"Ollie," he says. "He belonged to my ex."

Suddenly, I feel like a train is going through my head, my thoughts nothing more than echoing white noise and unstoppable force. I stop my picture-taking and shoot back up into a standing position. Without thinking, I blurt out, "You piece of shit." In a few steps I'm towering over him.

"Whoa, whoa, whoa." Al shrinks back but sitting on the couch, there's nowhere for him to go. He puts both hands up in front of his face as if to fend off an incoming blow.

"You're Alan?! *THAT* Alan?! I'm taking this dog with me. How dare you keep him from Vic?"

"Are you kidding?" Alan's voice is shrill with incredulity. "I've been trying to get Vic to pick up the dog for months."

"What." It feels as though the floor is lava beneath me, the room drifting around me, my stomach full of hot coals. "I feel sick," I say.

"Let me get you a glass of water." When Al comes back with the glass, I gulp it down as he waits for me to answer his million dollar question: "What did she tell you?"

The walk home is a blur. The anxiety I had on the way over is now multiplied ten-fold and blended with a rage the likes of which I haven't felt in a long time, maybe not since I was an angry teen. The loop in my brain is now simply, *She lied. She lied. Why did she lie?*

The stark feeling of betrayal has made clear something that now hurts too badly to admit: I was falling in love with her. And, admitting it to myself, I realize I was watching Gabby fall in love with her, too. *Fuck.*

I have more questions than ability to express them. My head is overwhelmed with cloudiness. I texted Gabby when I left Al's to tell her that I had something urgent and upsetting to discuss with her when I got home. I hope she's not too worried about me.

After a blur of time, somehow, I'm walking through the front door to our apartment.

"Honey, what happened? Are you okay?" Gabby launches to her feet from her spot on the couch upon my arrival. The look of worry on her face is enough to make me want to curse Vic out and tell her to ensure she never crosses paths with us again. My heart sinks at the thought of having to tell Gabby the truth about Vic, and I feel tears pricking at my eyes.

"I'm okay. I'm sorry I worried you," I rasp.

"Did this guy treat you poorly? I will kick his ass, I swear to God."

I know she would, too. I smile weakly. "No, no. the hookup was really nice, actually. The thing is, it's *who* I was hooking up with that I need to talk to you about." I take a deep breath and sigh. Gabby's eyes are as wide as saucers now, and she's gone so quiet I wonder faintly if she's holding her breath. "It was Alan. Vic's Alan."

"Oh, so I *do* need to kick his ass. Fucking jag. You should have just taken the dog back for Vic right then and there, honestly. Asshole!" She's talking a mile a minute, her voice a crescendo.

"Babe," I interrupt her gently, making myself meet her gaze. "Vic lied to us." My voice cracks around the words. This stuns her into silence again. Her eyes dart around the room as if she'll find an explanation among our furniture and tchotchkes, some kind of key that will make her understand what I'm saying.

"Al... Alan has been trying to get Vic to pick the dog up since they broke up all those months ago. Vic keeps dodging him. It's some kind of ploy to get him to want her to come back." I shrug, then add, "Not to be *that guy,* but he showed me the texts. He gave Vic the benefit of the doubt, even defended her to me, saying he understands that the breakup has been pretty hard on her. I don't know. I don't know. She lied to us, Gab, and I know you were developing some strong feelings for her, and honestly I was too..." I let myself trail off, noticing that now I'm talking a mile a minute.

I see Gabby's eyes turn glassy. She sighs, grabs my hand, and without a word, pulls me to the couch, where she lays her head in my lap. I don't know what else to do, so I just run my fingers through her hair.

 **32**

Gabby's Vertigo of the Heart

I'm crying on the couch with Darius. Flashes of red hair and soft skin and sweetness overwhelm my mind's eye. *Is it possible to have vertigo of the heart?*

"I don't know how to tell you this, but I feel kind of heartbroken," I say to Darius. "I was starting to develop real feelings for Vic. I was going to... I don't know, I thought maybe the three of us could *be* together."

"Me too," Darius says.

This makes me laugh a dark, incredulous laugh. "Really?"

"Yeah," Darius says.

"You were falling in love with her, too," I say. It's not an accusation. It just *is*. It feels true. Somehow, we were both falling in love with her.

Darius nods, and just repeats, "Yeah."

"What now?" I say. "We have to break up with her... or whatever."

"Yeah, we definitely need to talk to her," Darius agrees.

"I just don't understand why she *lied* to us. And doesn't she want her dog back? Can you imagine if we broke up and... I don't even know. I assume I'd take both of the pets, I mean, I had the cat when we moved in together and Mimi was my idea. Sorry, babe."

"I thought maybe we could do one of those shared-pet-custody modern arrangements, don't you think?" Darius says.

"That's gringo shit," I reply flatly. "I wonder what else she's lied about."

"Alan explained that the breakup was not mutual at all," Darius says. "It was all him, and she was really upset about it, even though he felt like things were flatlining for a while. I guess she was in denial."

"Honestly, it feels weird talking about her like this. She's not here to give her side of the story, a lot of it is speculation..." I start, but trail off, not even sure what I mean to say.

"I mean, yeah, but what else are we supposed to do? She isn't giving us a choice. When you lie, you destroy your credibility. I mean, I'll hear her out, but I'm not sure there's moving past this, Gab. I'm sorry. I can't be with someone like that, I can't even be *around* someone like that."

"Ayan," I say, my voice barely above a whisper. He knows what I mean just from those two syllables.

Darius takes a big, frustrated breath. "Yeah, this is some fucked-up déja vu." He scoffs.

Guilt creeps its way into my psyche. "I'm sorry I brought her into our life. I'm sorry I pushed us to this point. We were so happy, and I feel like I let her hurt us. This is my fault." I close my eyes and cover my face with my hands. It hurts to look at Darius right now.

"No, baby, no. It's not your fault. Hey, look at me." I shake my head, still buried under my hands, my attempt at hiding the new tears springing from my eyes betrayed by my sniffling. He continues. "I love you. There's no use living with regret, you know? We have each other. Fuck the liars of the world."

I uncover my face, unable to help myself. "Fucking a liar is what got us into this mess, hello...?" Darius cracks a smile and I feel a little better. "I love you," I say, guilt washed away by gratitude. Then, something dawns on me. "This is kind of weird, huh? We're like, going through a breakup... together?"

Darius chuckles darkly. "Yep, it's a new one for us. But I think we still need to do the actual breakup part, or whatever this is. We need to talk to Vic."

I roll my eyes. I am fully strapped in on a roller coaster of emotions, and anger is the next plunge I feel in my stomach. "I hate this," I say. "I hate that she made us think we had something so special together. What will she say about *us* now when we end things with her? There's no dog for us to '*hold hostage.*'" I make an air-quotes gesture.

A new thought slams into me. "Am I going to have to quit my job?" I lean into Darius' side.

"Honey," Darius says evenly, then runs a soothing hand across my hair. I sigh. "We need to talk to her. One thing at a time, okay?"

I can't handle lies. There's really nothing I hate more than a dishonest person, especially someone who uses their lies to tear someone else down. It's a stance I have never backed down from, because lies are weapons Darius and I are all too familiar with, because they were used against me, against us.

Darius and I didn't just meet in college by chance. We were introduced by Ayan, who was his best friend back then. Ayan and I knew each other in high school and then were lab partners in our undergrad environmental science lab. Bonding over pH strips and instruments neither of us humanities majors understood very well (he a Psychology major, me English), we became fast friends. Soon, we were studying together at the library, where I met his tall, handsome best friend with the intense, dark stare and the impossible lashes, Darius.

I fell hard and I fell fast, telling Darius what was practically my entire life story the first time Ayan cancelled on our group plans and we were left to hang out alone at a dive bar show. We ended up staying out late, him driving us through the streets of South Florida, windows down. That night, just learning the few things about himself he chose to share with me over late night fast food chain burritos, I was hooked on him, determined to learn everything about him if he would let me.

A few months into us dating, Ayan drove a wedge between us when he told Darius that I was in love with him and had confessed as much as recently as that week. He claimed I was just using Darius in an attempt to make him jealous. He later fessed up to his bullshit in the face of Darius' wrath and hurt at such a betrayal. At the time, I felt it was a disgusting lie, that he was jealous I had "taken" his friend from him (so stupid) or that maybe he harbored a crush on me. Now, with the advantage of hindsight and the wisdom from our experience with Vic, I wonder if Ayan had feelings for us both. It doesn't matter now.

Though Darius loosely stays in touch with him through his group of buddies, I never spoke to Ayan again, and at the end of this harrowing experience, Darius and I vowed explicitly to never, ever lie to each other. The years since have been peaceful, and thankfully, we learned to choose our friends more wisely. Honestly, I had almost forgotten the whole stupid, needlessly painful event.

Though Vic's lies didn't hurt us directly, and though the initial lie about the dog could almost be seen as silly in a certain squinting light, it's something I can't abide. If Darius hadn't insisted against it, I would be banging down Alan's door to apologize profusely for believing the slanderous shit Vic has been spewing against him. So much hurt, so many apologies owed.

By the time we're done talking and Darius heads over to his video game corner, it's late, but I still feel the ache to share with the only other person who knows my heart as well as he does. Sophie picks up on the third ring. I hear her TV in the background, which means I didn't wake her. She's not usually one to stay up too late, so I'm relieved I've caught her.

Given the rare late-night call, she doesn't bother with pleasantries. "Are you okay?"

A tendril of guilt shoots through my head in response to the worry in her voice. "Um, yeah, hey," I say, suddenly tongue-tied. "I just—" I get choked up all over again and burst into tears, blubbering half-coherent sentences that are garbled by my own sobs. Darius gets up from his spot in the corner and comes to me. I'm slumped over the arm of the couch, so he stands beside the couch and rubs my back in gentle circles.

"What happened?" Sophie asks patiently.

Finally, I manage to get myself together enough to say, "Vic lied to us." Apparently, that sentence is all the momentum I needed, and I'm able to power through a 30-second summary of the news Darius broke to me when he got home today. Somewhere around the 15-second mark, Darius resumes his position in the corner. I peek at him from my spot on the couch and catch him wiping at his own eyes as he slumps back down into his rolling chair.

"I know you feel like you're reliving the shit with Ayan from all those years ago," Sophie says, and her instinctive insightfulness surprises me a little, despite how well I know she knows me. I hadn't mentioned Ayan in my quick recap. "But he was a piece of shit, and from everything you've told me about Vic, she isn't."

"But she *lied*," I protest. "And it was a big one. Actually, it was a bunch of lies. I can't even count them all!"

"Yeah, but Ayan lied to manipulate you. Vic lied because she didn't know how to cope and basically had a little bit of a breakup breakdown."

"A little bit?" My incredulity sharpens my tone. "I can't believe you're defending her."

"I'm not," Sophie says. "What she did was not cool. I'm merely pointing out that she and Ayan are two completely different people, and these are two completely different scenarios," Sophie says, still patient. She yawns now. It's way past her bedtime at this point. "I guess what I'm saying is, if you want it to work with Vic, it can still work. But *only* if you want it to, if this is something you and Darius can forgive."

I huff an admittedly rude scoff at my best friend. "Goodnight, I love you," I say, my tone possibly the brattiest I've ever taken with her.

"Love you," she says, yawning and unfazed. I hang up, less heartbroken but more angry than when I called.

33

Vic's Love in the Park

I blow a little cloud of smoke into the verdant summer air, sitting on a bench at Schenley Park. A little weedy haze coats my nerves somewhat, but my foot is still bouncing with jitters. Gabby and Darius asked to meet out of the blue:

Hey, we need to talk to you. Can you meet us at Schenley today?

"We need to talk to you." The phrase echoes in my mind. There's no unserious way to take that, for better or worse. It's the *need* that makes it serious. *Isn't that always the case?* I joke to myself, thinking of all the times I've felt need for them, for their individual and collective touch, for their bodies.

Butterflies knock into each other in my stomach, a little stoned and more than a little excited. *Are they going to say they love me?* The hope reveals myself to me. After Hairy Pitts, I've tried to resign myself to not having any expectations. I love them, yes, but I can't just ask if they feel the same way. I may be healing, but I'm not ready to risk it all, to be rejected, to lose what I *do* have with them by greedily asking for more.

We've been so in-tune with each other so far, so the confidence that this could be what they have to tell me grows stronger. *That's what the* need *is.* So dramatic, I love it.

"Hey, Vic," a familiar voice says behind me, startling me out of my thoughts. It's Gabby. I feel a big smile bloom on my face and turn around.

"Hey," Darius says, standing next to her, eyes downcast. They're both wearing expressions I've never seen on them before. Serious, but something else I can't quite place that causes my guts to ball up into a pit.

My smile withers and I gulp my tiny spark of hope down dry. "Hey. Come, sit," I say, scooting over to one side of the bench to make room for them. Gabby sits beside me, Darius on the other end.

Gabby starts talking, fast, even for her. "I'm just going to rip it off like a bandage. We know you lied to us. Darius met Alan and we know he's not keeping Ollie against your wishes. You left him there. You insisted he keep the apartment. You left all your shit there." Every sentence is like a lash against my soul. What the fuck, Vic." She lets out a sharp breath as if winded, wounded. "You lied to us," she repeats.

Darius just stares at me, eyes wet with betrayal. I feel my own eyes start to burn.

"No, no, it's not that simple," I say. I want to defend myself, but I've been grappling with my own lies for nine? ten? months now. I don't know if there is a defense, if I even should defend myself. I take a deep breath and the sigh I let out turns into a twisted groan of frustration. I struggle to say what I haven't been able to even admit to myself. "I know I shouldn't have lied. Alan is a lovely person and I loved him very much. I couldn't accept the breakup, I couldn't accept... that he didn't want me anymore."

"What about us? Will you tell lies about us, too? What will you say at work to feed the gossip mill, that I'm a piece of shit? That what the three of us had wasn't real? I'm scared of you, Vic."

I'm scared of you. The words are like poison injections into my veins.

Finally, Darius speaks, and I hear hopelessness in his voice. "I know we never promised you anything, but I thought we had found something special together, the three of us. It turns out we were just placeholders while you pined for Alan."

I laugh darkly. "'Placeholders,'" I repeat. "You know, I thought yinz asked me here to tell me you love me. I was so excited." The words continue to bubble up. "I love you. I love you both." I look from Gabby to Darius until they blur, tears pouring over my vision.

"Please," Gabby says sharply. "You can't just announce you're in love with us and expect that to make it all better. We won't let you manipulate us."

"No, no," I collapse into myself, cradling my head in my hands in a semi-fetal position. It feels like my lies have cursed me into a spiral of misunderstanding. My own actions have invalidated my feelings, my credibility in expressing those feelings. I'm desolate. "I'm sorry I lied. I was in so much pain. I never thought he'd leave me," is all I can think to say.

"Thank you for your apology," Gabby says gracefully.

"Okay," I say, feeling as defeated as I did the day Alan left me. A question occurs to me then: "How did you even talk to Alan?"

Darius answers in a voice slightly above a whisper. "I met him on an app. I didn't realize he was your Alan until after we hooked up."

Hysterical laughter bursts from my throat and it feels like it belongs to someone else. "This is the most bizarre shit, I swear. This shit can only happen in Pittsburgh."

"It's not just *happening*, Vic. You caused a lot of this," Gabby says.

"I didn't *cause* Darius to fuck my ex," I snap back.

"He didn't know," Gabby retorts with a defensive fire behind her eyes that bores into me.

"I know, it's just a fucking lot. Jesus Christ," I curse.

"This would have been a totally different conversation if all that came to light from me hooking up with Al was that he was your ex," Darius says.

"Okay, but it still hurts to know that it happened," I say. "He's my ex, and our breakup is the hardest thing I've ever been through and made me feel very... undesirable." I wipe a tear from the corner of my eye and cross my arms in an attempt to hold myself together.

"Well, desire has nothing to do with us ending things between us. I think that's obvious," Darius says. "We just feel like we can't trust you. Embarking on not only a whole new relationship, but a whole new relationship dynamic, would be self-sabotage for us at this point."

"Okay," I say, feeling empty and tired. I wipe my snot on the neck of the old derby league t-shirt I'm wearing. "You know, I was going to tell you the truth in my own time, I just didn't know how," I explain feebly. "I'm gonna go now," I announce quietly, and walk away, unable to look at either of them anymore. They say nothing, but I feel them watch me go, feel the strong bond between them, their love powerful, even in the mundane act of sitting on a bench in the park.

I weep as I walk, not caring who fucking sees. The loss is so big, there's only one thing I want. My feet carry me to my old front door, where I knock softly.

When he opens the door, I can't look at Alan right away, but I finally do. "Darius talked to you," he says, not a question, not unkindly.

"I'm so sorry I lied about you. It was so fucked up. Please, can I take Ollie with me?"

"Thank you for your apology. And sure, of course. I was starting to think this day would never come," he says.

"I'm sorry, I was fucked up. I should have come to my senses a lot sooner. We should talk more, but I can't right now. I really just want to go home and be with Ollie and cry, okay?"

"I understand," Alan says, and my heart lurches in recognition of his familiar generosity in understanding and empathy as he invites me inside with a gesture of his hand, stepping to the side of what used to be our doorway. At the edges of my consciousness, I hope the love for him that was decaying in a corner of my chest can someday fertilize feelings of friendship. I realize for the first time that I would be honored to call him my friend, and that I couldn't see him as anything else anymore. The longing for him, for what we had, is a memory, a wound scarred over.

Upon walking into the apartment, I notice boxes everywhere. "You're moving," I say, echoing the tone of his own earlier non-question. I file the new information away to process later.

"Yeah, there's a pile of your stuff in the—" he starts, but he's interrupted by a little white flurry scrambling at my legs.

Picking Ollie up for the first time in the better part of a year, I cry harder than I have since the day I left. I cry into his fur, then hold him up to gaze into his dark, round eyes without a thought between them. He licks the air between our noses dumbly, my sweet angel.

Alan hands me his leash and harness from their hook on the wall by the door. "Thanks," I sniffle. I strap and buckle him in as Alan gathers a few essentials for him.

"Thank you so much for taking care of him. I promise, we'll talk about everything. I just don't have the head for it right now."

"Okay. I appreciate you coming to get him, though, and thank you again for your apology. It's a good step in the right direction for us to heal."

I nod, and he lets me out the door. On my walk home, I'm not crying anymore, though I know my face is quite splotchy. I smile at the familiar jingle of Ollie's dog tags making music with my footsteps.

 **34**

Darius and the Gift

I'm distracted in improv class during the stretch and share. When it's my turn, I just reach for the sky and say I'm rewatching my favorite comfort show and comment on how it's always nice to return to our personal classics, phoning it in.

There's a tightness in my chest. I can't stop thinking about Vic's tortured face the other day, contorted by the simultaneous vulnerability of her love confession with the heartbreak of the moment.

The walk home with Gabby was awful. We were silent, bumping arms softly every now and then, I think for comfort. That night, we cuddled extra hard, neither one of us wanting to feel alone. I woke up to her soft weeping once that night, found tears in the corners of my eyes when I woke up the next morning, and this morning. The debacle in the park is all so vivid, yet feels like a lifetime ago.

After going through the motions of warm-ups and suffering the mild embarrassment of missing cues or not hearing people talking to me, our instructor Sean asks us to take a seat so he can briefly go over today's lesson, which fundamental element of improv he'll be emphasizing in today's class.

"In improv, everything your scene partner does is a gift," Sean says, after briefly glancing at his lesson plan notes.

"If you initiate a scene by doing what you believe is 'planting crops,' but when your scene partner comes onstage, they say, 'Gee, this mining for rubies is really hard work,' don't correct them. Guess what?" Sean pauses for dramatic effect. "You're mining for rubies now."

Suddenly, my attention is back in the room. "Be generous with your scene partners, and you will benefit from their reciprocal generosity. Everything that happens on this stage goes two ways. So, try to remember in your scenes today: There are no mistakes, only gifts."

My heart aches with the overpowering wish for this statement to be true beyond this little local improv theater. *There are no mistakes, only gifts.* I consider the possibilities of shifting my perspective to view mistakes as gifts: gifts of enrichment, learning experiences, perspective... the possibilities are endless.

If nothing else, it feels good to be present in improv class again. For now, the tightness in my chest is replaced with an openness and excitement to meet my scene partners where they're at in the moment.

When I get home, I kiss Gabby hello and flop down onto the couch, snuggling up to her as she eats ice cream straight out of the carton. This alone isn't necessarily a heartbreak thing, just another Wednesday night. Her eyes and nose tell a different story, though. She's definitely been crying.

I rest my chin on her shoulder and open my mouth as I make a silly face, making stupid insistent noises until she spoons some ice cream into my craw with an unserious eye-roll, smiling despite herself.

"You're in a good mood," she says dryly, then feeds herself another spoonful of ice cream.

"Improv class was fun." I open my mouth to take my turn with another bite, then, mouth full, add, "Surprisingly deep."

She considers this with her next bite, listening with a thoughtful expression on her face as I continue. "Today, Sean talked about how there are no mistakes in improv. It's part of what helps improvisers think freely on stage. We're supposed to view any 'mistake' we make as a gift instead."

She feeds me another bite of ice cream and asks, "What do you mean, 'gift?'"

"Basically, we're supposed to turn everything our scene partner does into something... I don't know, positive." I consider my word choice. "Like, we can just lean into the mistake. There's something funny there, something to learn, something to extract or build upon... It actually got me thinking."

Gabby groans, her mouth full of ice cream. "I already know where you're going with this, and I hate it. You can't compare making a mistake in improv to lying in a romantic relationship."

"Why not?" I press, then open my mouth for another bite.

"Because! It's fucking bullshit. You said it yourself: How can we trust her?" Gabby turns her head to make direct eye contact with me, her big eyes even wider than usual with alarm and hurt.

"Well, I've been thinking a lot about what we know about Vic, and we know her pretty damn well. She's a good person. She acted from a place of pain. We all make mistakes, you know?"

"And how exactly is this mistake a gift?" Gabby cocks her head attitudinally.

"Honestly, I don't know that the mistake itself is a gift in this case, but I think that we can agree that Vic herself was a gift... is a gift. Having her in our life was really special."

Gabby sighs. "You miss her." She turns her head to look at me directly again, eyes searching mine as if trying to ascertain exactly what I'm feeling.

I nod. "You miss her, too."

"Yeah, but I'm scared. What if we break up and she badmouths me to the entire store?"

"She won't," I say. "You know she won't. She picked up Ollie right after we talked to her, based on when Al texted me. I think in this way, okay, maybe the mistake *was* a gift. She's learning from it, she will cope with a difficult situation or with heartbreak differently next time."

"So you admit that if we get together, it will end in heartbreak," Gabby prods.

I give her a stern look. "You know heartbreak is always a risk."

"It isn't with us," she says softly, a rare insecurity in her voice that makes my heart ache.

"No baby, no," I say tenderly, stretching awkwardly to stroke the top of her head with my hand. "I'm committed to you. We're committed to each other. But in giving my heart to you, I'm trusting you not to break it. And you're trusting me with yours."

"And you think we can trust Vic with our hearts?" Gabby sets the ice cream carton down on the coffee table. There's something desperate in her voice. "I love her, Darius. I do, but I'm scared. We don't know how the fuck to be polyamorous, and I feel like we did everything wrong before we even started."

"We'll learn. We'll educate ourselves, we'll listen and communicate with each other, and honestly, months of hot sex and bonding over mutual interests wasn't such a bad start." I nudge her. "I love her too, and it's really scary. I never in a million years thought that I could love a woman— *anyone*— other than you. And the fact that you love her too, and she loves us back... This is all just too special to throw away."

"If it were us, we would work through it. And she's part of us now. The three of us are the us." Gabby smiles and tears spill onto her face. She sighs and a small chuckle catches in her throat.

"If she'll have us, that is," I add. "The other day in the park was pretty intense. Maybe she decided we're too much, or maybe she wants a totally fresh start."

"Should we text her?" Gabby says.

35

Vic and the Happily Ever After

Darius and Gabby are coming over to my place. This time, their messages seemed softer somehow, though at their core they said they wanted to discuss something important with me, as they had said when they'd asked me to meet them that day at Schenley. Ollie watches me with a bored expression from his bed in the corner of my room as I throw on a slutty skirt and a cropped tank. I figure, you never know if they'll be feeling frisky, wanting one last hurrah for "closure" (I might indulge them), remind them of what they're missing if not. At the very least, I'll be damned if I don't feel hot when I'm in their presence.

I'm at my apartment, which is decidedly less shitty now that I'm actually allowing myself to settle in and add personal touches. Of the dozen I picked up from Alan last week, I only have a few boxes left to unpack. Ollie is happy as a clam and it isn't weird or sad living here on my own like I thought it would be. Though I liked the physical apartment I shared with Alan, it was always my vision and my touch that brought it to life, and nothing can ever take that touch away from me.

I try to keep an open mind before their arrival, not wanting to assume the worst. (What could the worst even be at this point?)

If they are coming for some kind of closure talk, I'm completely unprepared, but I don't have to distract myself from spiraling in my thoughts for long. An hour after my phone buzzed with flashback-inducing notifications from Gabby and Darius, they're at my door.

When they come in, I offer them Dr. Pepper, but Darius takes water and Gabby asks for coffee, of course. We exchange awkwardly formal and rote how-are-yous as I set the pot to percolate, then we sit down at my kitchen table, the dead pothos long gone and my unicorn planter moved to a cabinet for now. The coffee machine starts to sputter and drip, and the three of us stare at each other for a long moment.

"So... we're here to confess our love for you. No need to beat around the bush," Gabby says, somewhat sheepishly.

"Wow," I say, my heart leaping into my throat.

Darius clears his throat gruffly, and I wonder if he is feeling the same sensation I am. "I feel I should chime in to separately confess my love for you, since it feels weird to have Gabby speak solely on my behalf about it. I mean, I don't know, we've never both confessed our love to someone together."

The three of us giggle awkwardly, but I'm having trouble stringing words together. After that day in the park, I thought they would want nothing to do with me. Before I can string together a response, Gabby starts up again.

"Here, let's try this. I'll talk about how Vic makes me feel, only speaking for myself, then you take a turn and do the same. We really should have made a bit of a plan before showing up here,"

Gabby says.

"Improv, baby!" Darius answers in a goofy voice. Gabby rolls her eyes in feigned annoyance, affectionately.

"Vic... I never thought something as silly and fun and messy and filthy as a threesome could bring love, real love, into my life. Of course, you know I always thought Darius was the only one for me. And he *is* 'the one' for me, but... so are you. And I'm so excited to open up my heart in this way, I feel so lucky to have more love in my life." Gabby takes a breath, eyebrows raised as though she is bracing herself for what she is about to say. "Darius made me realize that one mistake, made from a place of difficulty and pain, shouldn't keep me from following my heart. You apologized to me that day in the park, and I accept your apology. I wasn't ready to that day, but I'm ready now, and I hope your heart is still open to loving me. I love you, Vic. I love your smile, I love your strong heart and filthy sailor's mouth, your mind, your confidence. I love making love to you, and I'd love to be your girlfriend."

"This is so extremely gay," I blurt out, and we all burst out laughing. My heart is soaring, but I want to let Darius say his piece before I try to make sense of the scrambled eggs in my head. I feel something hot awaken within me for the first time since I last slept with Gabby and Darius.

Darius takes a deep breath and sighs slowly, as if centering himself. "I'll pretend like Gabby's well-spoken poet ass isn't hard as hell to follow, um..." He chuckles, and I think I detect actual nervousness from the stoic Darius himself. "Vic, now that you're in my life, I can't imagine it without you. You are simply part of me, I carry you with me everywhere I go. I realized I loved you the weekend we went to your derby tournament. I felt so lucky to make love to the badass I watched on the track that day. I felt so proud of you and your talents, your passion, and I wanted so badly for you to call me yours. I love you."

I wanted so badly for you to call me yours, makes my panties absolutely soaked. Before my brain knows what's happening, I'm standing up out of my chair and then actually *on all fours* on my kitchen table. I don't know why, except I love a big gesture and I want nothing more than to get fucked by the two people I love on this table, to *make love* for the first time. I notice I have happy, overwhelmed tears salting my face as I kiss each of them deeply, passionately. I whisper into each of their lips, "I love you so much."

My head is a storm of thoughts. "We're like, a polyamorous throuple now, right? Committed to each other but then also open to new connections outside of just the three of us?" It feels as though I'm talking faster than I've ever talked, but I want to feel like I have some clarity as I plunge into the depths here.

Gabby and Darius nod and quietly mutter phrases of acquiescence, the smiles on their faces radiating an uncomplicated joy, as if all they want in their brief time on this earth is to kiss me and pleasure me and discuss our relationship dynamics. I'm so ready to enter a honeymoon phase with these two, to honeymoon with them forever, in endless, morphing iterations. Even now, all horned up and high on our feelings, it feels epically *real.* It doesn't feel like a fairytale at all, but instead simply, radically *as it should be.*

I'm at the center of a flurry of hands groping and kisses flying over skin, then Darius is behind me, taking full advantage of my ass' aerial position after checking in with me first. Gabby and I are engrossed in each other's kisses as I feel Darius hook my thong onto his finger and push it aside. The next thing I feel is his warm tongue in my folds, on my clit, and his thoughtful fingers pushing into me with intention.

When my knees start to ache, I twist to lay on my back, Gabby and Darius adjusting, clothes peeling off. From my position now flat on the table, I see in my peripheral vision that Gabby is walking into my kitchen. I hear her open the fridge. "What are you doing...?" I sing-song, trying to hint in my inflection that I might have some idea as to what she's up to.

A moment later, she's standing over me, glorious in nothing but her skin, holding a can of whipped cream. As she shakes the can, her tits jiggle from side to side and I think it's just about the most beautiful single image I've ever seen.

She positions the nozzle just above my mouth in a silent offering, and I part my lips into an open-mouthed smile to accept. She squirts a dollop into my mouth, and as she squirts another into hers, I give Darius an enthusiastic go-ahead for him to penetrate me with his hard length.

Darius and I hold each other's gazes with an intimate intensity I've never experienced with anyone else. His dark eyes are communicating deeply filthy, resonant, musical things to me that I don't think are possible to get across with words.

Gabby asks if she can sit on my face and soon I have the earth-shattering, perfect, tangy taste of her commingling with the sweet cream on my tongue. I'm in my happy place— no, I'm in *bliss*.

Food brought us together. Things got messy, but also sweet, and I absolutely cannot wait to keep making sweet messes of each other forever.

36

Epilogue

In the process of the store finally unionizing, Gabby and Vic, feeling a renewed sense of camaraderie and bondedness with their coworkers, confess to their extracurricular activities: their new relationship, their throuple with Darius. It turns out the rumor mill had been placing bets on the nature of their relationship since Gabby's very first week at the store, after much of the crew observed their chemistry, how they interacted with each other on the days Vic trained her.

In the end, those of the rumor mill who'd wagered the most cash were right, and the union deal they scored now protects their jobs and the benefits they've earned with their labor.

The happy triad moves into a little house they rent together near Highland Park, walkable to the store and an easy drive or bus ride to the bakery. Gabby was able to pay off her credit card debt, because polyamory is one of the most viable— if unlikely— ways for millennials to get out of debt these days. Her financial situation has improved enough that she is even able to get fancy manicures again.

While continuing to educate themselves on polyamory and

healthy attachment styles, the trio has even invested in a new-to-them couch! It was quite the adventure renting a van and moving it in, but they all fit comfortably on it cuddling and doing various other activities in pretty much any position. Sometimes, there's even room for Ollie and Mimi to cuddle on the couch, too, the two of them now BFFs (happily ignored by Groovy). Occasionally, the couch even holds other dates they bring home, ever-sturdy throughout each new experience.

Their life continues to be full of cakes, cannolis, and sweet, beautiful messes.

Acknowledgments

You just finished reading a book I wrote. Wow, thank you. My work never feels real to me until it reaches readers. Before that, it's just words and vibes strung together in my mind. So, thank you for making my work real, for making Vic, Gabby, and Darius and their love story come to life. Thank you for taking a chance on a brand-new indie romance author. I hope you'll hang out in my email list to see where the *Food Freaxxx* series goes next, and the other romances I'm cooking up.

Thank you to my husband for supporting my writing, always, and more importantly, supporting me as a person. You are the love of my life, my soulmate. Infinite besitos, my Darling.

Thank you to my writing community and all my friends and loved ones who continue to support me and uplift me, who nourish my spirit.

Thank you to Pittsburgh's queer community for dancing with me literally and figuratively for the past 7 years. Love yinz.

A special thanks to Becky and Andrée-Anne for making the cover of my dreams a reality, and to Casey Renee of Confections PGH for making the glorious *Messy* cake. It was as gorgeous as it was delicious!

About the Author

Corola De Rosa is a bisexual, Cuban-American style icon from South Florida. She is a Gemini who loves all things decadent. When she's not writing spicy romance, she's writing existential poetry.

Check out Corola De Rosa's website *coroladerosa.com* and subscribe to her email list for regular doses of decadence and updates on all things Food Freaxxx.

Indulgent: Food Freaxxx Book 2 **coming soon!**

Subscribe to Corola De Rosa's email list!